The Blue Amulet

A Novel

Mj Roë

Copyright © 2012 Mj Roë
All Rights Reserved

ISBN-10: 1475032196
EAN-13: 9781475032192

Library of Congress Control Number: 2012905294
CreateSpace, North Charleston, SC

This book is a work of fiction. Names, characters, places, and incidents are either products of the author's imagination or used fictitiously. Any resemblance to actual events, locales, or persons, living or dead, is entirely coincidental.

Visit the author's website at www.roezes.com
Front Cover Design by Brian Rollason "The Pixel Chemist"

For
Ben and Charlie

La vengeance est un plat qui se mange froid.
Revenge is a dish best served cold.

Anchored in the northernmost waters of the Tyrrhenian Sea off the Vieux Port of Bastia harbor, The Blue Amulet *was a splendid yacht. A modern technological wonder, with advanced satellite communications, a digital navigation system, global positioning system, and high-speed Internet connectivity, its sleek aluminum hull was adorned with a simple design. The light blue eye, familiar to the inhabitants of the Mediterranean region, had been bestowed on the magnificent floating palace by its owner to protect it against the dreaded curse of* le mauvais oeil, *"the evil eye."*

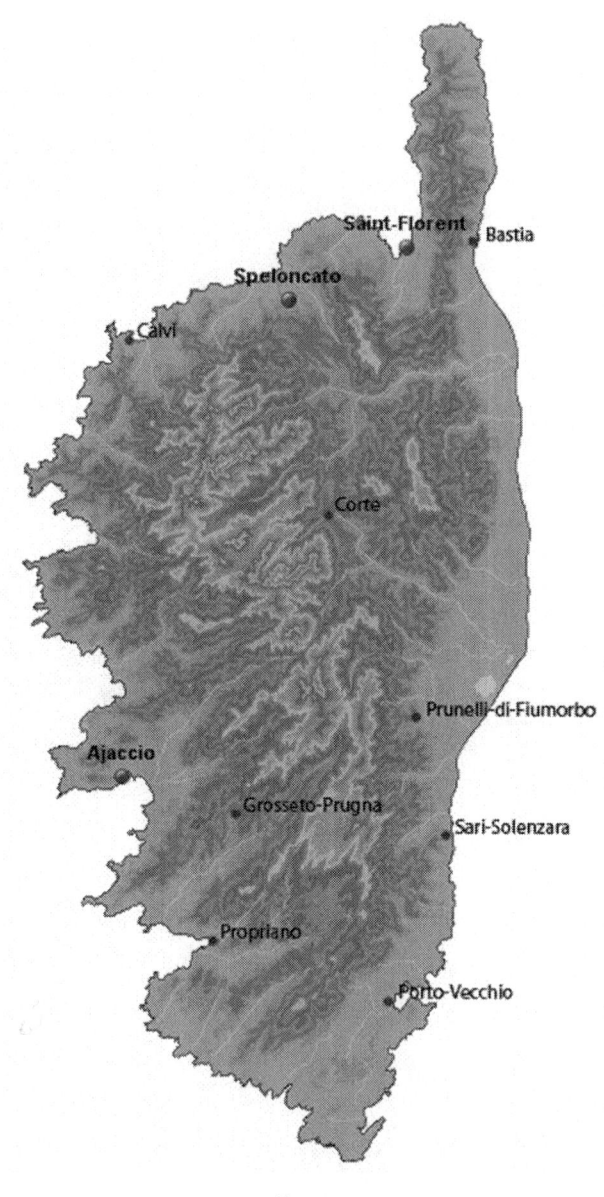

Corsica

The Blue Amulet
A Novel

Part One

CHAPTER ONE

Laguna Beach, California
August 1998

Mark Zennelli shielded his eyes and stared at the silhouette of the couple embracing in front him. Behind them, the Pacific Ocean sparkled in the bright afternoon sunlight. A feeling of quiet desperation overtook him. Anna Ellis had been the love of his life. Now, it was up to her. Had he done the right thing by telling her? The guy obviously loved her. What else could he have done?

Maybe I should have swept her away, he thought. *Taken her off to Catalina for the weekend, directly from the airport. Not revealed anything.*

A low growl came from the backseat of Mark's BMW convertible. Paris, Anna's golden retriever, was up on all fours, his tail on high alert, staring at the man embracing Anna.

"Easy, boy," Mark said as he got out of the car and grabbed the dog's leash. "She's okay. Well, maybe she's okay. I'm not so sure about you or me."

The canine growled again as Mark pulled him toward the building.

"All right. Come on. Let's get out of here." He led the reluctant dog along the side alley and up the rear stairs to his condo. As he opened the door, he turned to look back at the beachfront. The two were standing apart now, deep in conversation, and Mark could see that Anna was sobbing. He remembered with sudden alarm that she had said the Frenchman was dead, and she had seemed terrified when they drove into the alley.

Christ, he thought. *Dead? What was all that about?* He raked his hair nervously. *It's all that Diamanté's fault. Him and his terrorist brother.*

Chapter Two

With my heart telling me to turn back toward Laguna Beach, I drove up the coast of California in a rented car that sparkling August afternoon in 1998.

My gut hurt every time I thought about Anna, leaving her with the impression that I never wanted to see her again. It wasn't true, of course. I loved her more than I had loved anyone in my life, which was why I had to leave her. I knew she wouldn't be happy living under an assumed name, possibly on the run, nor could I, in all consciousness, have asked that of her, a well-known author. What would have been the point of taking all that away from her?

Tired, hungry, exhausted emotionally, and with a lot of decisions to make, I decided to stop and spend the night in Carmel-by-the-Sea. That evening, I sat on the beach, watching the sun set. As a cool breeze gently whipped the cypress trees along the rugged coastline, I made a plan. I had the money to make it happen, having secreted my wealth away in a bank account in Switzerland no one but I knew about. I would have to use it discreetly, of course, and I would have to be careful that my whereabouts not be discovered. As I pondered my new name,

Charlie Guilbert, and how I would have to get used to it, the sun slipped below the horizon, and the air chilled. I took a sip of wine and noticed, farther down the beach, the dark figure of a man who appeared to be watching me.

Part Two

Chapter Three

Strasbourg, France
Three years later

Mark Zennelli stared straight ahead with a scowl on his face. The group seated with him at the huge wooden conference table looked as bored as he. A balding man with an unruly fringe of Einstein-like white hair, the presenter, stood before them at the head of the table. The room smelled of stale cigarette smoke.

Christ, Mark thought as he loosened his tie with his index finger and tugged at his shirt collar, *why does it have to be so freakin' hot in here?*

The presenter paused to glance at his notes. A distinguished-looking, dark-haired man in wire-rimmed glasses seated next to Mark seized the opportunity to raise a question. His loud voice startled the dour group, and heads and eyes rose suddenly in unison, conveying a marionette likeness.

Mark poured himself a glass of water from the pitcher in front of him. He drank it in one gulp, then pushed his chair away from the table. It was no use. He couldn't stand it any longer. He politely excused himself and walked out into the hall.

The entire length of the corridor was enclosed in glass. It was raining, and the wind blew the water in sheets against the panes so that the view of the bronze statues in the courtyard was a dark gray blur.

At least, he thought, tugging at his collar again, *it's cooler out here in the atrium.*

One of the women in the meeting had followed him into the hall. He turned and smiled in recognition. She returned the smile.

"Some boring presentation, *non?*" she said.

"Christ! Yes," he responded, shaking his head. "Where did they find that guy anyway?"

She laughed. "Brussels, I think."

Mark slowed and waited for her to catch up to him. "By the way, Sophie, do you know a really good admin who is looking to relocate? Like, I mean, to California? I'm losing Jacks in a month. She's marrying someone from Montana, or Wyoming. Somewhere like that. She's so in love that she's leaving L.A. and *moi*." He pointed to himself with a glint in his eye. "Anyway, the firm needs someone who speaks French this time around. I think you understand why."

"Actually, *oui*." She winked at him. "I've someone in mind, too. I'll give her a call first to see if she's interested." She pushed open the women's restroom door and glanced at him over her shoulder. "See you back in the meeting."

He nodded with a salute as the door closed behind her. He wasn't going back to the meeting, if he could help it. Well, maybe for the wrap-up. He had promised his thoughts on the approach to the client. Another bunch of bullshit. That's all these things were, a bunch of bullshit.

He walked over to the window. The clouds were dark and heavy, and he could see that the early September storm wasn't letting up yet. He looked at his watch and calculated the time difference. It would be a little after midnight in California. Anna would be sleeping. He had wanted her to come to Strasbourg with him, but no, she said, she couldn't because her agent was negotiating rights for her latest book, and she couldn't go anywhere right now.

"You would pass on a trip to Strasbourg, for Christ's sake?" he had asked her.

Never, since he had known her, had she refused an opportunity to travel to France.

She was vague for days about her reasons for not going. It mystified him. Then, yesterday, two hours before his flight took off, as she climbed into the car to drive him to LAX, she finally confessed the truth.

"Mark, there's something I haven't told you," she said, backing the BMW out of the driveway a little too fast. *"The real reason I can't go with you is...is, well, I have some news."*

"You got a movie deal for your book?"

She'd laughed. *"No. Better. I'm pregnant."*

He was thrilled.

"This is wonderful, gorgeous! Why didn't you tell me before?"

"I just found out this past week for sure, but I've been suspicious. It's definitely not as easy as it was with Luc, though. I'm nauseated all the time. The reason I can't go to France with you is that I'd be sick all the time."

Thinking about her now made Mark wish he had immediately cancelled his trip. Anna was everything to him. He had married her in Obernai, coincidentally just a few kilometers from Strasbourg, in October 1998. Their third anniversary was coming up, and he was planning on surprising her with a piece of jewelry he was going to pick out in New York City on his way home. He planned to get Luc a special new toy, too, at FAO Schwarz. Mark smiled as he thought of Luc. The handsome, curly-headed two-year-old wasn't his biological son, but he loved him as his own. A soft wave of warmth ran through him. He'd have another baby to adore now. Maybe a little girl.

Mark's thoughts were abruptly interrupted by a sudden commotion in the corridor. He glanced behind him as two security guards rushed past and disappeared quickly around a corner. Briefly wondering what that was all about, he decided to turn back toward the conference room.

"Hey, Mark!" The call came from one of the meeting attendees, a young Ethiopian dressed in a white tunic and white pants, a brightly colored scarf draped over one shoulder. "We're about to wrap up, man," he said with a wide grin. "Don't want you to miss out."

Just at that moment, alarms sounded, and security guards with guns arrived. Everyone in the meeting was ordered to evacuate immediately.

"What the hell's going on?" Mark asked as they were quickly herded out of the building and into an underground tunnel beneath the canal.

"Rumor has it's a bomb threat," said the man next to him. "We get those all of the time."

Mark ran his hands through his hair. His heart was beating fast. *Holy shit,* he thought, looking around him. No one seemed to be in a state of panic. *How can these people act so freakin' nonchalant?* He definitely was not used to bomb threats.

When the all clear came, they filed slowly back into the conference room. Damp and cold, Mark took his seat and poured himself a glass of water, thinking that at least he wasn't hot anymore. When the meeting resumed, he cleared his throat and began a series of seemingly well-thought-out comments on the entire proceedings, adding his personal set of conclusions, and finally standing and moving to the grease board to list for them his specific recommendations. The group nodded in agreement, and Mark thought to himself, *What a bunch of bullshit*. He was ready to go home.

Chapter Four

Laguna Beach, California

Anna Ellis Zennelli stood on the balcony of the second story of her home overlooking the Pacific Ocean. The marine layer hovering over the coast was thick, and the morning air was cool and filled with the excited cries of seagulls searching for their breakfast. She frowned as she pulled her shawl around her shoulders. Maybe she shouldn't have told Mark about the baby like that. Maybe she should have waited until he returned from France.

She sighed as she went back into her office and sat down at the PC. She wasn't at all happy the way things had been going with her writing recently. The new book, titled *The Princess and the Doctor*, had been published, and Anna's agent, Harry, had told her it would be a huge success. Sales, however, had so far been lackluster. It was the story of a discreet love affair carried on by Diana, Princess of Wales, and a French doctor whom she meets during her many journeys to Africa. Despite Harry's efforts, Hollywood hadn't bought off on the film rights either. At this rate the movie probably would never happen. Worse yet, she didn't have an idea for another story.

Life with Mark, on the other hand, was joyful. He truly made her happy. The thought of him being in France now without her made her feel sad. He had asked her to go with him. She knew he wanted her to go. The two times previously they had been in Strasbourg were wonderful, romantic trips. The first was just a month before they had become engaged; the second was for their wedding in Obernai. What had made her turn down the chance to go back to France now? Was it really the pregnancy? Or was it because she didn't want to be reminded of C-C? Now, as she always did when she thought of Charles-Christian, she wondered briefly where he was, what he was doing, then dismissed the thought immediately.

The phone rang. She let it ring. It was probably her mother-in-law. Viola and she had never hit it off truly well, but they tolerated each other for Mark's benefit. What irked Anna was Vi had been making the most pointed remarks about Luc recently.

"Isn't it strange, Anna? I can't see Mark in him at all." Then those beady Italian eyes would drive into hers like a couple of daggers.

Anna always responded with a sweet smile and a shrug. What could she say, anyway? She and Mark had made a pact not to reveal the true nature of Luc's conception. *"If it doesn't matter to me,"* Mark had told her, *"why should it be anyone else's business, including my mother's?"* Anna had loved him for that.

Luc played next to Anna's desk. The child giggled and held up a toy car for her to appreciate, his dark gray eyes shining like a pair of iridescent Tahitian black pearls. Anna smiled at him. *What a beautiful baby he is*, she thought as she rubbed her belly and a sudden wave of nausea hit her. She had a feeling the second one was going to be a girl.

Chapter Five

Sophie Chen watched Mark Zennelli appreciatively as he exited the Villa Schutzenberger in Strasbourg's European Quarter. It was early evening. The rain had stopped, but the street in front of the Villa was still damp, and droplets of water dripped from the leaves of the trees. He was an attractive man, Sophie thought. There was no doubt about it. Probably in his late thirties. Slightly graying sandy hair, well built, expensively dressed. She hurried to catch up to him.

"Hey, Mark. Wait," she called out.

Mark slowed a bit.

"Are you headed back to your hotel?" she asked.

"Yeah. Think I'll walk since the rain has quit. I feel like I need some exercise and fresh air."

"Want to have dinner later? Unless, you have other plans, that is."

"No, no plans," he said. "Sure, why not. There's a couscous restaurant just around the corner from the hotel. Don't know the name, but I hear it's pretty good. Want to meet there, say in a couple of hours?"

"I know the restaurant. Sure. Meantime, I'm going to do some shopping before the boutiques close. Bye-bye."

She winked at him flirtatiously as she darted down a side street.

***

Mark followed Sophie with his eyes. She was young, slim, long legged, dressed in a black coat and boots, a light gray pashmina wound around her neck, her pitch-black straight hair pulled back into a severe ponytail. *One of those French-Indochina beauties*, he thought. He watched her until she disappeared around the corner.

"Careful there," he said aloud as he looked at his Rolex. It was early morning in Los Angeles. He had just enough time to walk back to the hotel and call Anna before dinner.

***

"I've your new admin for you," Sophie said later as Mark held the chair for her at a linen-covered table in the restaurant.

"Really? That fast?"

"*Oui*. I told you I had someone in mind, didn't I? She's a friend of mine, actually, from Toulouse. She's been dying to go somewhere, anywhere, just to get out of Toulouse. I called her, and she's faxing her curriculum vitae to me. I think she's a little overqualified for an admin job, but maybe she can work her way up in your firm."

"Overqualified?"

Sophie grinned. "She's a lawyer."

Mark shook his head. "No good," he said, raking his hair with his fingers. "It's a small firm. Damn, I can't afford to pay lawyer's wages for an admin."

"You won't have to. Gabrielle will settle for whatever your Jacks was making, plus the cost of the flight to the States."

"You're kidding."

"Told you she wanted out of Toulouse badly. Anyway, I'll have the fax from her later on this evening."

Mark handed her his card. "Tell her my partner at Zennelli and Zennelli, my sister, Adriana, will be in contact. She's the one who's mostly in town. I'm traveling all the time.

Sophie took the card, seductively touching his fingers and looking him in the eyes as she did so.

Mark felt his face flush. He cleared his throat and concentrated on the menu in front of him.

"The house specialty sounds good," he finally said.

When the waiter had taken their orders and poured them glasses of the house wine, an Alsatian Gewürztraminer, Sophie smiled and held up her glass in toast. "I'm so glad tomorrow is Saturday, aren't you? Are you doing anything?"

"Actually, I'm flying to Paris. Meeting my dad there. Sunday we're both headed for New York. Back-to-back meetings all day Monday in Lower Manhattan."

Sophie made a little pout. "Too bad," she said, leaning over the table toward him. "In that case, want to stop by my hotel a little later for a nightcap? We can discuss Gabrielle's qualifications some more."

There was no mistake; she was flirting outright.

"Sophie," Mark said seriously, looking straight into the beautiful hazel eyes with a slight epicanthic lid, "I'm a married man, and I'm in love with my wife."

Sophie Chen laughed as she took a sip of the wine. "And so you are, Mark Zennelli. I'll try to remember that."

Chapter Six

Paris, France

Mark Zennelli's father, Romano, or "Zenn," as he was known in Hollywood circles, was not a pretentious man. Affable and warm, he had been brought up by hardworking Italian immigrant parents and had made his way in Hollywood with perseverance and dedication. He was the kind of person who made friends easily and was quick to include them in his inner circle along with his wife, Viola, their two children, Mark and Adriana, and his large extended Italian family. Despite his wealth and position, he had very few enemies and was well connected most everywhere in the world.

As he rode in the taxi past the Eiffel Tower, Romano Zennelli was eagerly anticipating the next few hours when he would have his son all to himself. Even though they both lived in the Los Angeles area, he had not spent much quality time with Mark in the past three years. When they discovered that their separate business trips would place them in Paris on the same weekend in September and, coincidentally, in New York City for meetings the following Monday, they had made plans to go out for dinner in Paris on Saturday evening and then fly together to New York the next day.

As the cab pulled up in front of the apartment building in the seventh arrondissement, Zenn looked down the street. He loved this arrondissement and this apartment. He and Viola had picked out the piece of real estate in 1997 so they would have a place to stay on their numerous trips to Europe. Viola had decorated it, and it was stylish and comfortable. It already had a nostalgic air to it. Mark and Anna had stayed here the weekend they became engaged, and Adriana had come here to study law.

As Zenn opened the door to the apartment, his cell phone rang. It was Mark.

"Hi, Dad. Just landed at de Gaulle."

Zenn smiled. "I just got in myself. Really looking forward to seeing you, son. Your mother is jealous. She wanted to be here, too."

"Hey, Dad? I've got some super news to tell you, but the shuttle is here. Got to go. Meet you in an hour or so at Le Meurice. *Ciao*."

Zenn stood in the foyer of the apartment. A ray of sunlight shone through the stained glass window. He smiled. "Super news," he said, repeating Mark's phrase. Those words could only mean one thing: a celebration was in order.

Chapter Seven

New York City

Early Tuesday morning, Romano Zennelli awakened in his room on the thirtieth floor of the New York Marriott Financial Center Hotel. His head was spinning, and his stomach felt off. When he tried to get out of bed, the nausea set in. Breaking into a clammy sweat, he picked up the phone and dialed Mark's room.

"I think I've come down with the stomach flu, or maybe it's food poisoning," he said, trying to think what he'd had for dinner the evening before. "You'll have to handle the meeting this morning for both of us. I'm not going to be able to make it farther than the bathroom."

"Can't we postpone?"

"If we postpone, we lose the deal. Simple as that. You've got to represent us."

Mark groaned. "Okay, but if I screw up, you'll be sorry."

"You'll do just fine, son. You can fill me in on all the details later. By the way, my cell phone's battery is dead and I've misplaced the charger, so don't bother trying to call me. I'll meet you at the airport at one. *Buona fortuna!*"

***

In California, Anna was in the kitchen preparing Luc's breakfast. The phone rang. She looked at the clock, then frowned. It was 6:30 a.m. What was her mother-in-law calling about at this time of morning?

"You're up early, Vi," she said as cheerfully as she could, cradling the phone against her shoulder to pour another cup of coffee. "What's up?"

Viola's high-pitched, panic-stricken voice filled her ear. "Are you watching the news? There's something going on in Manhattan."

Anna froze. Mark had called her just an hour before. He was scheduled to attend a breakfast meeting before heading for the airport and flying home. He had told her how much he loved her, and then he had said, *"Hey, gorgeous, I've been thinking. I hope we have a girl. I think we should name her Isabelle. Love that name. What do you think?"* The last thing she had heard before they were cut off was *"I'll call you before my flight."*

She'd not thought much about it. Cell phones did that all the time.

Grabbing the remote, she quickly turned on the TV and stared, not comprehending immediately. There was a great deal of smoke pouring from one of the twin towers of the World Trade Center.

"What's happened, Vi? I didn't have the TV on."

"Oh my God," Viola said, panicked. "A plane hit the World Trade Center. The North Tower. They're trying to get everyone evacuated. I can't reach Zenn and Mark on their cell phones. *Dio mio!*"

"Mark called me earlier. Maybe about an hour ago. We were cut off. He and his dad were supposed to have a breakfast meeting in the restaurant…" Anna stopped talking and put her hand to her mouth in horror. "Oh my God, Vi," she gasped. "It was supposed to be in the restaurant on the hundred-sixth floor of the North Tower."

Anna heard Viola scream.

"Stay calm. I'll try to reach Mark again. Call you back."

Anna hung up immediately and quickly dialed Mark's cell phone number. It went directly to his voice mail. She tried again.

"Mark. Answer, please, Mark. Answer," she pleaded aloud over and over, but there was no response.

The phone rang again. She picked it up quickly, her hand shaking. "Mark?"

"No, it's me," Viola yelled. "I was hoping you had reached him." Viola was so panicked Anna couldn't understand the string of half Italian, half English that came next.

"I'm sure they're okay, Vi." Anna tried to reassure her mother-in-law, but she herself could hardly breathe as she watched the scenes being broadcast live from New York on the morning news. "I'll keep trying. It may be just a cell problem. Will call you if I can get through."

Anna stared at the television. Suddenly, she had a sickening feeling in the pit of her stomach, a dark feeling of foreboding she had felt before in her life. The first time was just before her grandparents had died.

***

In New York, Romano Zennelli awoke to a deafening explosion. Not understanding immediately what was happening, he opened the curtains and peered out his hotel room window. The September sky was crystal blue. In the distance, he could see smoke pouring from an upper floor of the North Tower of the World Trade Center, and, in the street below, fire engines and police cars racing to the scene, their sirens blaring. As Romano watched, he heard the roaring sound of an airplane overhead. Alarmed, he pulled the curtain open further and looked up. He saw a plane, a passenger jet, flying low and circling uncomfortably close to the buildings.

"*Madonna mia!*" Romano muttered to himself as he watched the plane fly directly into the side of the South Tower. He looked at the clock on the end table and tried to think. Where was Mark? Maybe he was back from the meeting by now. He went over to the phone and called Mark's mobile. No answer. Frantic, he quickly dressed, ran into the hallway, and pounded on the door to Mark's room. No response. A group of people stood waiting for the elevator, anxiously pushing the button.

"They don't seem to be operating," a woman said impatiently.

Romano ran down the hallway, pushed open the door to the stairwell, and barely touched the steps as he flew down several flights of stairs to the ground level.

In the street, the noise of beeping fire trucks and police sirens was deafening. Hordes of screaming, desperate people ran in all directions. Some carried crying children; others frantically yelled into their cell phones. A man ran by him shouting, "There's a bomb!"

Zenn's nostrils filled with dark black smoke and dust, and his eyes watered. He heard another huge explosion, and splinters of debris rained on him. In vain, he called out Mark's name as he tried to push his way through the chaotic scene.

***

Nine months later, following the birth of her baby girl, Anna added an entry to her journal.

Within hours, the twin towers of the World Trade Center collapsed in the worst terrorist attack on United States soil in history. The phone call Mark promised me prior to his flight home never came. It would be weeks before his father, Romano Zennelli, would be able to speak of the event, and he never forgave himself for setting up the meeting that sent his son, my beloved husband, to his death. I fear I will never learn exactly what happened that day.

On May 11, 2002, Isabelle Adriana Zennelli was born. Her father's remains have not yet been recovered.

PART THREE

CHAPTER EIGHT

Bastia, Corsica
August, 2002

Four years ago, as Charles-Christian Gérard, village doctor in Castagniers, France, I was involved in a historical event that will generate suspicion, conspiracy theories, and questions for decades. Because of the top-secret nature of my involvement, and the possible danger to me if my knowledge of the event were to be leaked, I was given a new identity and told to go make a new life for myself. Thus, my name became Charlie Guilbert, and, despite the fact that I was not a fugitive, I felt like one.

For three years, I wandered the globe as a member of Médecins sans Frontières, doing medical work in Africa, in the sub-Saharan countries, and elsewhere, whenever natural disasters occurred. After the devastating Gujarat earthquake in northwestern India in 2001, I had had enough. Feeling the need to settle somewhere permanently, I chose my father's native Corsica for my new home. With no clear plans for the future, but with my mind made up, I put my finger, on impulse, over the map of the island and closed my eyes. Fate pointed me to the port city of Bastia in the northernmost region.

I was five years old when my father first took me to visit Corsica. He and I traveled to Ajaccio, where he was born. Though I was very young, I remember well the rugged terrain and the scent of the *maquis*, the rich vegetation that covers the entire island.

Bastia is old and truly charming, in a weathered sort of way. Some call the port "shabby chic," because of its tall, faded buildings surrounding a marina full of posh yachts, but when I arrived here, I was immediately taken by the wrought-iron balconies, the narrow alleys I could get lost in, the crumbling golden-gray walls overgrown with *maquis*, and the Corsican music I heard coming from shuttered houses with half-open jalousies.

In Bastia, my life became much like the routine I knew as an emergency room physician at la Pitié-Salpêtrière Hospital in Paris before the events of August 31, 1997. I worked nights at the central hospital, Centro Ospedaliero Generale, and slept days in a small apartment nearby. *Voilà tout. J'ai existé.* I led a Camusian existence. Were it not for a new acquaintance, there would have been little diversion.

I had been in Bastia only a short time when I first met Nicolos Manos, or Nicko (pronounced "Neeko"), as he preferred to be called. Younger than I by a decade, well built, and charming, he was a man few people could resist. A complex blend of playful extrovert and dark pessimist, he had curly black hair, thick eyebrows, piercing dark brown eyes, and a stubble of a beard. He never ceased to catch the attention of the locals in town, especially when he drove his expensive Italian-built motorcycle very fast through the narrow streets. He drank wine from the bottle and danced Zorba-like dances at all hours. When asked, he said he was Greek, but once admitted to being half Corsican, his mother having come from a small town in the interior. He said he traveled a lot on business, but, curiously, he never said what business he was in. I never told Manos anything about my own life prior to arriving in Bastia, and he never asked me about it. It is the Corsican way, not to ask, so I, in turn, did not ask him.

Two weeks prior to our first encounter, Manos glided into the old port on a magnificent yacht named *The Blue Amulet*. He anchored it in the harbor for a day or two, and then sailed out. The locals talked about that eye-catching boat for the next week, and then, to their amazement, it sailed into the harbor again. This time, Nicko showed up at the emergency room at Centro seeking medical attention for a bad cut to his forehead. That was when I met him. I sutured the wound, and he invited me to dine with him on the yacht that evening. From then on, every time the yacht arrived in the port, which was weekly, Nicko invited me aboard. He liked to party, and his guests were encouraged to stay overnight on the yacht. In my case, he even gave me, for my own personal use, a key to one of the six guest staterooms.

Nicko was very proud of that yacht. And no wonder. Greek built, it was a floating mansion, two hundred feet in length, with enough technology on board to qualify it as a first-class military surveillance ship. He was very protective of it, too. Hence, he explained the design of concentric black, light blue, white, and dark blue circles painted on the prow. Nicko wore a blue glass amulet of a similar design hanging from a leather cord around his neck. When he was asked about it, which was often, he explained that it was bestowed upon him when he was a baby to ward off the evil eye from others. In the case of the yacht, he said, the staring eye on its prow was supposed to bend a malicious gaze back to the originator, thus putting up a protective shield.

On a rainy night recently, I left the hospital emergency room at half past midnight. Nicko had invited me to a late dinner with some friends, and as I waited for him in the wet, deserted street, I wondered which of his several girlfriends would be with him. The Greek was seldom without a beautiful woman on his arm for the evening and in his bed for the night. As was usually the case, we planned to have a few drinks in town followed by dinner and dancing on his yacht.

"Heh, Charlie," I heard Nicko calling as he rounded the corner, one arm draped over the shoulders of an attractive young woman, and the other holding an umbrella over her head. "Ready for a little fun?" He was grinning. "How about it, eh *mon ami*? A bit of Διασκέδαση?" The word was Greek, meaning "amusement." He used it often.

I smiled and extended my hand. "*Bonsoir,* Nicko. *Ça va?*"

"*Ah oui. Comme toujours*, as always," he said, slowly angling his head downward as he undraped his arm from the young woman's shoulders to shake my hand. "Meet my new *petite amie*, Marthe." He returned his arm to its spot and brushed his lips seductively against the woman's cheek. "*Orea*, beautiful Marthe," he said breathlessly, devouring her with his eyes. "This is my good friend Charlie." He flashed his wide smile. "He's sort of shy with *les filles*. I've been trying to find the right match for him."

I laughed, held my open hands out from my sides, and said, jokingly, "My arms are still waiting, Nicko."

What Nicko didn't know was that I loved someone, and I ached always when I thought of her, but I didn't confide that to him or anyone.

The woman that night was typical of Nicko's taste, not mine: long black hair, overly thick false eyelashes, short skirt, very high heels, a sturdy figure, muscular legs. I noted that she was almost as tall as he.

"*Bonsoir*," she said, demurely, but she wasn't French. The accent was German.

"Come on, guys," Nicko said, swinging Marthe around. "Let's get out of this rain. I'm *kéfi* tonight."

I knew, from experience, when Nicko said he's *kéfi*, meaning "in good spirits," we had a party to go to.

Chapter Nine

Southern France
Near the city of Grasse

The ornate wrought-iron gate opened to reveal an exquisite country mansion complete with red tile roof, vine-covered golden stucco walls, green window shutters, and red geraniums in boxes perched on the windowsills. Anna Zennelli stopped the rental car in the Italian pine-lined driveway. She checked her image in the rearview mirror, glanced at her sleeping children in the backseat, then opened the car door and got out. A pomegranate-colored bougainvillea poured over the garden wall, and the musky, heady scent of roses filled the air. As she stood with her hands on her hips, admiring the scene, the big wooden front door opened and Anna's good friend Monique emerged, followed closely by her husband, Georges.

"*Les voilà! Coucou!*" Monique sang out as she waved her hand in excitement. "*Chérie*, you're here!" Monique ran to Anna, threw her arms around her, and kissed her on both cheeks.

"You look wonderful, Monique."

With her short-cut brown hair, long neck, and fine-boned face, Monique always reminded Anna of the French film star Juliette Binoche.

"*Enfin*! I was so anxious and worried," Monique said. "How are the children?" She peeked into the backseat. "Oh, *les anges*! Georges, look! Such angels! They're both sleeping."

Anna laughed. "They weren't such angels on the plane. Luc, especially, was a handful."

Georges greeted Anna and kissed her on both cheeks. Then he helped her lift the toddler from his car seat without waking him and carried him into the house.

"Oh, *quelle frimousse*!" Monique said, peeking into the baby's carrier. "What a sweet little face! I can't wait until you see the adorable bassinet I found for her to sleep in."

Anna followed Monique into the house. In the center of the large foyer, a huge blue-and-green ceramic vase filled with tall bearded irises sat on an oversized round wooden table.

"The bastide is indeed beautiful, Monique. Just as you said."

"Isn't it! We've named it Beausoleil. A wonderful name, *n'est-ce pas*? Remember, *chérie*, the photos I showed you? How run-down it was when we bought it? It's taken most of the past four years to get this much done, and there's still a lot more to do. Sometimes, I get exhausted."

Anna yawned. "Speaking of exhausted," she said.

"You need to get some rest, *chérie*. Go on upstairs and make yourself comfortable. Later, I'll give you a tour, and we can catch up. Second door on the right at the top of the stairs. It's almost an apartment it's so large. I want you and the children to think of this as your home for the entire month."

Georges descended the stairway. "*Et voilà*," he whispered to Anna, smiling. "I managed to put *le petit* to bed without waking him. Here, let me carry the baby up for you." He lifted the baby carrier from Anna's arms.

"You two are wonderful," Anna said as she followed him up the stairs. "I'll never want to leave."

"We hope you will be comfortable here," Georges said. He handed over Isabelle and opened the door for her.

The room was decorated in the blue and yellow textile colors of Provence, and there were bouquets of lavender and roses set on the desk and mantel. Two huge beds with big, fluffy comforters and oversized bolster pillows dominated the center of the room. Luc was sleeping peacefully on one of them. To the right were French doors, which opened onto a patio with a large potted lemon tree.

Anna put Isabelle in the ruffle-trimmed pink bassinet, closed the door, and sat down on a small white sofa. Despite being dog tired, she was grateful that Monique had nagged her about making the trip. *"France is where you can find* le joie de vivre *again,"* Monique had kept saying.

Monique and Anna had been best friends since the two were students at Paris University IV, the Sorbonne. Anna had stayed many times with Monique and Georges in their elegant apartment on rue Beaujon in Paris. In 1998, after she had learned she was pregnant, she had flown back to them in a state of panic. Desperate to help her, Monique had secretly called Mark, and, of course, he had arrived on the next plane.

Anna recalled the scene now. She had burst into tears when she saw him. *"It's okay, gorgeous,"* he had said, enveloping her in his strong arms. *"We'll deal with it."* Then, later, in Montmartre in the rain, he had proposed to her on his knees. They had married in France, in Obernai, then returned to California for a grand wedding reception at his parents' Bel Air estate.

The house overlooking the Pacific Ocean, inherited from her grandparents when they died in a car accident in 1997, became Anna and Mark's home.

Tears welled in her eyes as she thought of her grandparents, the loving couple who had raised her after her mother had died. Her father, the French-Corsican soldier whom she never knew, had been killed in the last days of the Algerian War. In 1997, she had learned that his father, her grandfather Diamanté, was still alive, and she had finally met him the following August. She would see him again this trip, as he and his wife, Elise, lived in the small village of Castagniers, not far from Beausoleil.

Thinking about Diamanté, she got up and walked out onto the patio. A soft summer breeze caressed her cheekbones. It carried the sweet scent of roses and lavender from the garden below, reminding her of another rose garden, and C-C's house, also in Castagniers. She sighed heavily. *What has become of him?* she wondered. *Does anyone even know where he is?* So many questions, and now some new ones since Mark's death. *Would C-C want to know about Luc? He is, after all, the boy's father. If so, should I try to find him?* The tears spilled from her eyes. In the short period of four years, she had lost the two men she loved.

A whimper from the room brought Anna hurling back to reality. She hurried inside, gathered the hungry three-month-old into her arms, and kissed her.

"Beautiful Isabelle," she said as she scooped up a bottle from her carry-on. "Let's have something to eat."

Chapter Ten

Strasbourg, France

Adriana Zennelli walked at a brisk clip toward the offices of the European Union in Strasbourg. This was her first trip representing Zennelli and Zennelli since Mark's death, and she wasn't certain what was ahead of her. To the client, it had been portrayed as a meet and greet to introduce her, but it was more than that. In going through the file of correspondence with the Strasbourg client, she had discovered discrepancies serious enough to warrant further investigation. It was the main reason for making this trip. She had to get to the bottom of what had been going on. The question still nagged her: how much did Mark know? She checked her watch. She was already ten minutes late. Well, that would make an excellent first impression. Silently cursing at her high heels, she picked up her pace. Why had she worn stilettos anyway? What was she thinking? These cobblestones were murder. As she entered the building, another woman caught up with her.

"You must be Adriana," the woman said, extending her hand. "I'm Sophie Chen. I knew your brother. I've been looking forward to meeting you."

Adriana turned to the attractive woman standing next to her. "Yes, I'm Adriana Zennelli. Mark mentioned you," she said, shaking the woman's hand. "Pleased to meet you."

"I'm so sorry for your family's loss. He was well respected around here."

"Thanks," Adriana said softly. "Losing him was a terrible blow."

Sophie nodded sympathetically. "Come," she said, taking Adriana's elbow. "Let me introduce you around."

"I'm so late. I'm going to make a terrible first impression," Adriana said.

"Not at all. We don't get underway until all the pleasantries are over, including the croissants and coffee." Sophie led Adriana through the glass entryway. "Incidentally," she said, "do you still have a position open for an admin? Last time he was here, Mark and I talked about your interviewing a friend of mine for a job with his firm."

Adriana had completely forgotten about that. Mark had left her a message on the office phone very early the morning of September 11 suggesting she get in touch with someone about the open admin position.

"I'm sorry," Adriana said. "Mark did give me a name to contact. With all the events in the days after the attack, I completely forgot. She lives in Toulouse, right?"

"Yes," Sophie said. "Her name is Gabrielle, and she is still looking for the right opportunity, preferably in the States. She desperately wants to leave Toulouse. Her boyfriend left her recently, so she's more anxious than ever."

Adriana handed Sophie her card. "Have Gabrielle give me a call while I'm in Strasbourg. It might be perfect timing. My sister-in-law and her children are in the South of France for the month. I'm planning to visit them before I leave for California. Maybe I can travel through Toulouse to interview your friend on my way."

"That would be terrific. Well, here we are." Sophie guided Adriana into the conference room. Several people were standing around drinking coffee. "Prepare yourself," she said with a wink. "These meetings can get pretty boring."

Adriana recalled a phone conversation she had had with Mark. How was it he had summed it up? A bunch of bullshit. That was it. She put on a smile and set about introducing herself.

Chapter Eleven

Beausoleil

The sun hung low in the sky, and a mild evening wind carried the strong scent of jasmine from the valley below. Anna and Monique sat in cushioned wicker chairs on the back patio admiring the incredible palette of colors that made up the magnificent vista. In the distance, a shimmering copper-gold sliver of the Mediterranean Sea sparkled along the horizon.

Monique took a sip of her wine and sighed. "This is my favorite time of the day," she said. "It's so serene, and the *parfum*. I love the scent of the flowering trees. It changes from month to month. Every time we come here, it's different. In May, it was orange blossoms and roses."

Anna took a deep breath. "I'd like to visit the perfume factories in Grasse while I'm here," she said, propping Isabelle on her shoulder to burp her.

Georges came out of the garden shed, followed closely by Luc and the Durochers' two dogs.

"I'm going to teach Luc how to play the game of *pétanque*," he said, holding up a box of groove-patterned steel balls.

Anna watched Georges show Luc how to toss the balls onto the grass. She was reminded once again of the huge hole the loss of Mark had made in their lives.

"Mark's suitcase arrived just before I left," she said.

Concerned, Monique put her hand on Anna's shoulder. "Oh, *chérie*. It must have been terrible."

Anna took a deep breath. "It was found later at his hotel, all packed. There were toys he had bought for the children, and this bracelet..." Her voice trailed off as she thrust her wrist out for Monique to see the diamond-encrusted gold cuff.

"So they haven't discovered his body yet?"

Anna shook her head. "They are doing DNA testing. The medical examiner has warned us that there are some remains that may never be identified."

"Where was he, exactly? Do you know?"

Anna stared out over the valley. "Mark's father had set up a last-minute breakfast meeting that morning with a new client. Mark was to accompany him. All I know is that Romano became ill, so Mark attended the meeting alone. The restaurant was near the top of the first tower that was hit. Romano took it really hard."

"The poor man."

Anna looked down at Isabelle. The child had fallen asleep. "There was a message left on Romano's cell phone," she continued, her voice cracking, "from Mark." She shut her eyes tight, trying to stop the tears from spilling. "Romano didn't pick it up until days later. Mark said if he didn't make it..."

Luc came running up to Anna. He held up a small wooden ball for her to see. "*Cochon*, Mama. *Cochon*," he said, pointing to the ball. "Uncle Georges said it's a *cochon*."

"That's right, Luc," Anna said, quickly wiping her wet cheeks with the palm of her shaking hand. "It's called a pig."

"Peegie...co...co...cochon." The three-year-old squinted at her, then smiled and giggled as he ran off.

Monique handed Anna a tissue. Then she got up and took the sleeping infant from Anna's arms. "You were saying, *chérie*, about the message Mark left?"

Anna blew her nose. "I've listened to it over and over," she said. "There was a lot of background noise, but his words were clear. He said, 'If I don't make it out alive, take care of Anna and the children for me. And never stop telling them how much I loved them...'"

Tears welled in Monique's eyes. She gently touched the fine golden hair and ran her index finger along the baby's soft pink cheeks. "It's just all so sad," she said, kissing Isabelle on the forehead. "This beautiful child will never know her father."

Anna stood and took a deep breath. She lifted her chin to stare at the hazy blue sky above. "I've got to move on, Monique. I know I have to, but I keep thinking about the past. Including C-C."

"I never did like that man," Monique harrumphed, blowing breath from her lips.

"Yes, I know, Monique, but he is Luc's father."

"And you don't know where he is."

"Correction, Monique. I won't ever know where he is."

"*Bon*. He left you. Then why think about him?"

Anna didn't respond. She merely shrugged her shoulders and sat down again.

"*Tiens*, you look so haggard and thin, *chérie*. I'm thinking that we could make it a bit easier for you this weekend..."

Monique hesitated, then continued, "I mean, when you go to Castagniers to see your grandfather Diamanté. Perhaps Georges and I could take care of Isabelle. Then you would only have Luc to be concerned with, *non?*"

"I don't know," Anna said, shaking her head reluctantly. Monique's proposal had taken her by surprise. "It's wonderful of you to offer, but I can manage with the two children."

"*Et alors*, consider it, *chérie*. Our chef's wife, Marie-Thérèse, raised four children of her own. She's here with Pierre, and I know she would be delighted to help us. You don't have to make up your mind now. It's just that you seem so exhausted. I worry about you."

Anna stared at her friend. Monique was correct. She did feel worn-out, emotionally and physically. Perhaps a couple days' break from taking care of the baby would do her good.

"Well, I'll think about it," she said.

Anna had a lot to think about. She had to figure out how she was going to tell her grandfather Diamanté about Luc, and then there was Jacques, C-C's father, and all the unanswered questions about C-C himself, to which she suspected only her grandfather could provide some answers.

Chapter Twelve

Route D614 became narrow and winding as it twisted and climbed its way to Castagniers. Anna came to a bend in the road, pulled over, and she and Luc got out of the car. They looked out over a dramatic vista softly visible through the summer haze. Below them was a sheer drop to a ravine. Beyond it, tranquil villages with terra-cotta roofs dotted the soft green hills, and vast acres of lavender planted in long parallel lines filled the valley. A soft breeze tossed Anna's hair.

"What do you think about all this, little guy?" she asked her son.

Luc looked up at her. The cold set of his dark gray eyes reminded her of C-C. With his curly dark hair and olive skin, he was a miniature version of his handsome father. "I want a cookie, Mama," he said, frowning into the sun.

The two of them climbed back into the car. Anna dug through her bag and handed Luc a treat.

The drive into Castagniers was just as Anna had remembered. Surrounded by hills, the small village stretched out along a single paved street. In the center of the sun-drenched town square was an elegant stone fountain crowned by an artichoke and surrounded by flowers. At one end of the square was the *mairie*, the eighteenth-century town hall, with the Tricolor flying over the front entrance. The café, her grandfather's café, which he had named the Ajaccio for the capital city of Corsica, was directly across. Several patrons were seated at outdoor tables under the shade of large green umbrellas. Anna parked the car in the velvety shade beneath a plane tree. A low chiming of bells in the distance drew her attention upward to the slim two-story-high carillon tower of the vast Cistercian convent that dominated the hillside. She took a deep breath.

"This is Castagniers," she said, unbuckling her seat belt. "And that"—she pointed the café out to Luc—"is the Ajaccio."

Elise, her grandfather's wife, was on the terrace, arranging small bouquets of bright golden sunflowers in blue glass vases. Her vivid blue eyes sparkled when she saw Anna, and she began waving. Behind her stood Anna's paternal *grand-père*, Diamanté Loupré-Tigre. It had been four years since Anna had met the septuagenarian. She had never forgotten the first time she saw those dark, piercing eyes, and the deep scar extending upward from his right temple under the black beret.

Elise hastened toward the car, her arms wide. "*Oh là,* Anna, *bienvenue*," she said in welcome. "We've been watching for you, *n'est-ce pas*, Lobo?"

The two women embraced, air-kissing both cheeks, French style.

Anna noted that the Portuguese Elise still lovingly called her husband "Lobo," a reference to his vulpine-like gaze that had given him his *nom de guerre*, *le Loup*, "the Wolf," in the French Résistance.

Diamanté came forward with a shy smile on his face. "*Comu sì?*" he said in Corsican. "How are you?"

"Oh, *Grand-père*," she said tearfully as she gently embraced his hands. "I am so glad to see you."

Diamanté kissed her forehead. They held each other tightly for a long while.

"I've brought my Luc to meet you," she said finally as she stepped away and lifted the boy from his car seat. Luc held on to Anna tightly and hid his face shyly against his mother's shoulder.

"*Mais*, Anna, where is *le bébé?*" Elise exclaimed, peering into the car.

Anna put Luc down. "She's with Monique and Georges, Elise. It's just Luc and me this visit. I'll bring Isabelle next time."

Elise made a moue, showing her disappointment.

The café dog, a mixed breed with long, floppy ears and soulful eyes, came from behind the bar, stretched its front legs, and limped over to greet Anna, his bushy tail making windmill circles in the air.

"Oh, Max," she said as she bent down to rub the dog's ears and was awarded multiple wet, sloppy licks on the face. "You survived after all!" She looked at her grandfather, questioning.

Diamanté cocked his head sideways. "The old boy was lucky."

Luc patted the dog's head. "Nice doggie," he said with a giggle, his shyness forgotten.

Anna stood and surveyed the restaurant. The green awning on the old building sported a new sign in bold white letters: Bar Tabac Restaurant Chambres d'hôtes Ajaccio.

"You finally did it?" she exclaimed. "You added the bed-and-breakfast?"

Diamanté chuckled. "It was at Elise's insistence. When I objected to the idea, she argued the name Ajaccio derives from the Roman *adjaccium*, meaning a place of rest. So I gave in, reluctantly."

Elise beamed. "*Oh là!* Let me give you a *petit* tour," she said with pride. "It's so different from when you were here four years ago."

"You two go ahead," said Diamanté as he lowered himself to Luc's level and put his gnarled, arthritic hands on the boy's shoulders. Luc was staring at him. "I want to get to know my great-grandson better."

"Mama," Luc said suspiciously, "what he say?"

Anna realized Diamanté's heavy Corsican accent was difficult for the little boy to understand.

"He wants to know you, Luc," she assured him. "It's going to be fun. Why don't you two play with Max?"

The old mutt recognized his name, and his tail wagged youthfully.

Diamanté stood and asked in English, slowly so Luc would understand him, "Do you want to see a secret cave?" Luc's eyes widened. "It's in the wine cellar." Diamanté held out his hand, and Luc reluctantly took it.

"Wine cellar, Papa?" he asked.

Anna smiled. Luc had called Diamanté "Papa." "You've got a new name now, *Grand-père*," she said.

"*Oui*, and I like it, too," Diamanté replied, his black eyes twinkling. Then he whistled to the dog to follow. "*Bon. Viens*, Max. Let's show the secret cave to Luc."

Anna watched as they disappeared through a heavy wooden door behind the zinc bar. Then she took Elise's arm, and the two of them went into the restaurant.

"He seems well, Elise," she said. "You both look wonderful. You are obviously good for each other."

Elise shrugged and raised her eyebrows. "*Ouf!* We are getting old, Anna. Lobo has developed a slight cough, which worries me, but the doctor says it is nothing." She stopped in the center of the restaurant and put her hands on her hips, surveying the room. "As you can see, the *resto* has been updated."

To Anna, it seemed unchanged, but she said, "It looks wonderful, Elise." Then she asked, nervously glancing in the direction of the kitchen, "Is Jacques here?"

"*Oh là, non non*. We haven't seen him in over a year. He had a bad time after...after, well, you know. His heart is no good." Her eyes grew wide. "We thought he might die, but he survived." She held her hands out from her sides and shrugged her shoulders.

"Where is he?"

"In Corsica. The northern part. I don't recall just where exactly. My memory is getting bad. We heard he has opened a *resto*."

Anna heaved a huge sigh of relief. She would be able to avoid the inevitable confrontation with C-C's father, at least for now.

CHAPTER THIRTEEN

Early evening

Candles twinkled on the patio table as the setting sun cast shadows across the mountains. The perfume of roses and the scent of herbs from the Ajaccio's garden mixed with mouthwatering aromas from the restaurant's kitchen. From the dining room came the muted sounds of clicking silverware, whispered conversation, and a lone violin playing a medley of romantic French music.

"I can't tell you how much I have wanted to visit you," Anna said to her grandfather as she relished the scene. Four years before, this same piazza had been the stage for a celebration in honor of his and Elise's wedding. A few days later, it had provided the setting for a fatal altercation between him and his half brother. In horror, Anna had witnessed the angry exchange, the threats, the dog, Max, lunging at the intruder, and the subsequent gunshots.

"There are so many memories," she said now. "I can't ever forget your lovely wedding, the wonderful food, the Corsican dances, the stories."

"Especially Jacques's story," Diamanté added with a chuckle. "Do you remember it?"

"The duck story?" Anna laughed. "How could I forget?"

"Ah, *oui*. It was *superbe*, the celebration," Diamanté said.

Anna noted the glint in his eyes.

"If only it had ended there," she said. "I had nightmares for months about the night before I flew home."

Diamanté patted her hand. "We had to get beyond those memories, too." He looked at his wife. "*N'est-ce pas, chérie?*"

Elise nodded, wrinkling her nose in a smile. It was she who had saved Diamanté's life that night. "It has been difficult sometimes for us, but working on the *chambres* and setting up the bed-and-breakfast has been good. Plus, we had the house to redo, too. You will have to come tomorrow to see it."

"I'm not sure if I'm ready, Elise."

Diamanté looked at Anna. "We understand. Charlie put a lot of effort into that house. You probably wouldn't like seeing it so changed."

"It's not that. I'm sure it's beautiful…" Anna's voice trailed off. She took a sip of wine. "There is…something…" She cleared her throat. "I want to tell you."

The two old people stared intently into her eyes, baffled by her sudden change of tone.

"It's…it's that…you should know that Luc is C-C's son."

"*Chì?*" Diamanté asked in Corsican, his eyes wide. He put his hand over his mouth to catch a sudden cough. "*Mais*, I don't understand, Anna," he said. "Charlie's?"

"It's true. I was pregnant when I left here."

"*Oh là!* Did Charlie know?" Elise asked, cupping her cheeks with her hands.

Anna shook her head. "He had left me by the time I..."

Diamanté coughed again. This time, the cough was followed by a slight wheezing sound as he struggled to regain his breath.

Anna gave her grandfather a concerned look, but Elise shook her head as if admonishing her not to react.

"Were you aware he came to see me in California, *Grand-père?*"

Diamanté lowered his eyes. "*Enfin, oui,*" he said, cautiously. "I was informed of it."

"So you knew he wasn't killed in the accident, then? When did you learn that?"

"Anna, I can't tell you anything. A few days after you left Castagniers, I received a call." He removed his beret and rubbed the scar on his forehead, a signal that something was troubling him. "I was astounded, frankly. Apparently, there was a double."

"Did Jacques know?"

Diamanté shook his head. "He was told the body couldn't be identified. They closed the coffin, and he never saw anything."

"But—"

Diamanté put up his hand as if to warn her to stop the interrogation. "He's Corsican," he said sternly. "We Corsicans don't question."

"Doesn't he deserve to know the truth now?" she persisted. "How can it be fair to have kept this from him for four years?"

Diamanté's eyes were moist. He shook his head. "*Désolé,*" he said. "I'm sorry. It wasn't my decision, Anna."

The three of them sat in silence. The air was cool. A chorus of croaking frogs serenaded them in the darkness, and garden lights twinkled in the tree above.

A man emerged suddenly from the side pathway along the vine-covered wall.

"Ah, *monsieur,* Muranaka-san. *Bonsoir,*" Elise greeted him.

"*Bonsoir,*" the man replied. Then, seeing he was interrupting a private dinner, he bowed low and said apologetically in halting Japanese-accented French, "*Oh...excusez-moi. Je me suis trompé.* I must be mistaken. *J'ai cherché le restaurant.*"

"He's a guest," Elise explained to Anna. "It's his first evening here."

Diamanté rose from his chair. "*Par ici, monsieur. Je vous y amène.* This way, sir." He took the man's arm and guided him toward the dining room. To Anna and Elise he said, "I'll just show him to his table. I'll be right back."

The man bowed again in the women's direction.

When the two were out of hearing range, Anna whispered to Elise, "So you know about C-C, also? That he wasn't killed, I mean?"

Elise smiled. "*Oh là,* Anna, Lobo had a nightmare one night. He awoke and started talking about Charlie not being dead. I thought he was still dreaming, but he was awake. He told me after that. Maybe it was because we were in Charlie's house. Everything, right after especially, was Charlie's. Even the dog. You remember how Max followed him everywhere?"

Anna nodded. "Max was definitely C-C's dog."

"*Eh bien*, Lobo told me Charlie had gone to see you. I tell you, Anna, he has not shared more information with me than that. I don't even know if he himself ever saw Charlie again."

"And he's not going to tell us if he did, obviously," Anna sighed.

"What exactly did Charlie say to you? I know he loved you. It was always obvious. He must have given you a clue."

Anna shook her head. "He told me nothing, Elise, other than he had to go away, forever, and I couldn't ever see or talk to him again. It wasn't long after that when I found out I was expecting his child."

The two women were silent when Diamanté returned, carrying a platter of cheeses, which he deposited on the table in front of them.

"Try the Bûchette de Banon," he said, pointing to a small log-shaped cheese nestled in the center. "It's *chèvre* from Provence. Very mild and creamy."

Anna cut off a small portion and placed it on the plate in front of her.

"This may seem direct, *Grand-père*," she said as she tore off a piece of crusty baguette, "but do you think you could ever find C-C?"

He stared at her. His dark black eyes grew cold. "*Enfin*, I'm not active anymore," he said, evading her question.

Anna persevered. "When C-C came to see me in California, he said he had to assume a new identity. Isn't there some way to locate him? A child is involved, *Grand-père*," she pleaded, "a child who needs his father."

Diamanté's eyes softened. "Do you want to find him, Anna?"

"I don't know. Truthfully. But I think Luc should be given the opportunity to know his father. And, C-C should at least be told he has a son."

"I don't disagree, *ma chère*, but…" Diamanté said, hesitating. "*Zut*. I have to be honest with you. We may never be able to learn what became of him."

Anna's own dark eyes pierced his. "For Luc's sake, we've got to try."

"Lobo," Elise interjected, "Jacques should be told about Luc. He is, after all, the boy's grandfather."

Diamanté rubbed the scar on his forehead again. "I think you are right, but we need to bear in mind that he has had a hard time. For him, Charlie is dead, buried in Rouen four years ago. He is like a hot-tempered bull, my old Corsican friend. I can't predict how he will react to the news of a grandson."

Anna clicked her tongue, adding, "All the more potentially explosive since he never much cared for me, if you recall."

Elise pressed on. "Why not go to Corsica? Take Luc. Show him his roots. Anna should see her father's grave. You always say how much you want her to see it, Lobo."

"Do you want to go to Corsica, Anna?" he asked.

"Yes," she answered. "But only for a couple of days. I can't leave the baby with Monique for too long."

Diamanté looked from Anna to Elise. His wife nodded her head in encouragement.

"*Bon*," he said, resolutely tapping the back of his knuckles on the table. "*On y va, alors.* We go then to Corsica."

Chapter Fourteen

The morning sky was azure blue, and a soft breeze fanned the small group of guests who were seated under the shade of umbrellas at outdoor tables in front of the Ajaccio.

Diamanté opened the car door for his great-grandson. "*Tiens,* Luc, do you want to go on a boat ride?"

The little boy climbed into the car seat, his head bobbing up and down enthusiastically.

Elise came forward and lovingly cupped Diamanté's cheeks in both hands. "*Bon voyage, mi* Lobo," she said, then wagged an index finger at him. "Remember, those curves are dangerous." She turned to embrace Anna. "Keep an eye on him. He drives too fast."

Anna smiled and climbed into the car. "Are you finally going to tell me what our itinerary is, or am I to be kept guessing?" she said to her grandfather.

Diamanté adjusted the rearview mirror, started the car, and waved to Elise. Once they were underway, he said, "We'll take the ferry from Nice to Bastia. It's a five-hour trip. The boat is comfortable, modern, like a cruise ship. I rented a cabin so Luc can have a nap en route."

From the backseat, they heard a small voice say, "No, Papa. I don't want to take a nap."

Anna winked at Diamanté.

"*Et puis*, and then, we travel to Speloncato tomorrow," he continued. "It's a bit of a drive, over an hour, but you will experience the fragrant undergrowth known as the *maquis*."

"The original name for the Résistance during World War Two."

"*Exactement*. Appropriate, too, coined in Corsica, where the movement began, for the dense hillside undergrowth that covers the lowlands."

"Is Speloncato where the graves are?"

Diamanté nodded.

"What's it like?"

He raised an eyebrow. "I haven't seen the village for a long time, Anna. It's very old, sits on a mountaintop six hundred meters above sea level. My father, Jean-Pierre, was born there, as was my mother, Tesa. They are buried alongside my brother, Ferdinand, my wife, and our son, your father. He hesitated for a minute, coughed, then cleared his throat. "The cemetery you are going to see is not unique for Corsican villages," he said. "We have a family tomb. I will be buried there someday, too."

"What was my father like? I read his journal from the war. The one you gave me when I left France after your wedding. It's so sad and insightful. I couldn't put it down."

"He had a way with words," Diamanté said with pride.

"He planned to be a professor after his military service?"

"*Oui*. He was fascinated with history. He probably would have written several books, too. He definitely wanted to write."

"Did he have any girlfriends?"

"Oh, he had a few. None serious, that I recall." He looked over at Anna. "Your mother was no doubt the love of his life."

"I think something went wrong between them before he left California. She may have thought he left her for good. There were several comments in his journal to the effect that he had to right something between them after the war. Too bad he never got the chance."

"Did Stu like him?"

She shrugged. "My grandfather never said. As I told you, it was very brief. He was dying and hardly able to talk when he told me about him."

"Then we'll probably never know."

"Tell me about your wife."

"Ah, she was a pretty one, my Clotilde." Diamanté glanced in her direction. "Dark hair and eyes like yours. We started our first restaurant together. In Ajaccio. It was a lot of work, but she never complained. I loved her very much."

They had reached the ferry landing in Nice.

"Let's go explore our boat, Luc," said Diamanté as he grabbed the little boy's hand. "It's going to take us to Treasure Island."

***

The ferry approached the port of Bastia in late evening. Standing on the deck, Anna, Diamanté, and Luc were welcomed by a flock of *chee*-ing, swooping seagulls and a strong scent.

"It smells like thyme and rosemary," said Anna.

"The scent of the *maquis*," Diamanté said, and he inhaled deeply. "There's nothing in the world like it. You know you are approaching Corsica when you smell that."

As it entered the harbor, the ferry glided past a very large yacht. The sleek boat was lit up like a hotel. Anna studied it, fascinated.

"What is that?" she asked Diamanté, pointing to a design painted on the yacht's prow.

Diamanté stared at it, then said, "It looks like a blue amulet. It's a common symbol in the Mediterranean. There's a lot of mystery surrounding it. People think it protects them."

"From what?"

"*Le mauvais oeil.*"

"The what?"

"The evil eye. Individuals thought to be most capable of casting it, unintentionally or at least unconsciously, supposedly have blue eyes."

"Hence, the blue circle?"

Diamanté nodded. "It's a belief that goes back as far as Roman times. Whenever something valuable, or attractive, becomes suddenly, inexplicably indisposed, it is assumed to have been 'eyed.' The only protection is the amulet. Don't be surprised, Anna, if you see some of the locals mock-spitting like this." He demonstrated: *phtoo, phtoo, phtoo*. "It is customary, when admiring something or someone, to do so to ward off ill will."

Luc started to laugh. "Ho! That's funny noise, Papa," he said, then attempted an imitation: *phtoo, phtoo, phtoo.*

"Now, Luc," Anna scolded, "spitting is not nice."

"But Papa did it." Luc pouted.

Anna gave Diamanté a mother's version of the evil eye. "Look at all the boats, dear," she said, trying to divert the boy's attention by pointing toward the old port. Its weathered and crumbling buildings were aglow in light, providing a perfect backdrop for the mass of illuminated sailboats and fishing vessels bobbing in the murky waters.

"I'll go get the car," Diamanté said after the ferry had docked.

Luc grabbed his hand. "I want to go, too."

Anna stared at the waterfront, wondering fleetingly if Diamanté had shared the entire itinerary for this trip with her.

Chapter Fifteen

During the hour-and-a-half drive to Speloncato, Anna was reminded of the hairpin turns and steep, serpentine roads of Southern France. The terrain, she noted as she watched out the Fiat's window, was much more mountainous and rugged. With Diamanté driving at race-car speed, they headed west on D81 to the N197 and finally to the D63.

In the backseat, Luc was glued to the scenery, pointing out pigs and cows along the roadside. "Look, Mama," he said excitedly as they swerved around a sharp curve. "Goats!"

Diamanté braked suddenly, and hard, throwing them forward in their seats.

As they waited for the herd to cross the road in front of them, Anna's attention was drawn to a mountaintop village just ahead. Against the lush green backdrop lay densely packed stone houses with tile roofs, clustered around a single church with a steeple and bell tower. Bathed in the afternoon sunlight, the whole village had taken on a soft golden hue.

"Is that Speloncato?" she asked.

"*Oui. On arrive.* See that house under the single pine tree?" Diamanté pointed to the southwest. Anna nodded. "That was the house my mother was born in."

Low stone walls covered with creeping thyme lined the sides of the winding road. They entered the village, a labyrinth of narrow streets, stairs, rock walls, and small gates. Diamanté parked the car near a fountain in the shade of an olive tree. Across the center square, they could see a tiny café with two tables surrounded by green-slatted chairs. A hand-painted sign above a small stand under the awning advertised *Glace*. A woman and two small children were licking ice-cream cones.

"I want ice cream," Luc announced, his eyes wide.

"Me too," Anna agreed.

"*Eh bien*," Diamanté said with a laugh. "I think I'd like some *glace*, too." He opened the car doors for them. The midday air was hot and still. From inside the café came the faint sound of an accordion playing Corsican dance music.

"On the way back to Bastia," Diamanté said to Anna, "we stop in Saint-Florent."

Anna looked at him suspiciously.

Diamanté removed his beret and scratched his forehead, then continued, "At Jacques's restaurant."

"You've tricked me!"

"*Pas du tout*." He coughed, then shook his head indignantly. "Saint-Florent is on the D81, only twelve kilometers from Bastia. We drove past it on our way here."

Anna recalled Diamanté pointing out the small town at the foot of Cap Corse in the Gulf of Saint-Florent. The Saint-Tropez of Corsica, he had called it.

"You didn't tell me Jacques was there," she reprimanded him.

Diamanté looked confused. "You wanted to tell him, didn't you, about Luc?"

"Well, yes..." she hesitated. "I thought you were going to do that."

"It is best, *ma chère*, if we do it together."

Anna bit her lip. So that was the part of the itinerary he hadn't told her about earlier. She should have guessed.

After they had had their ice cream, Diamanté led them along a cobbled pathway behind the church. "The cemetery is this way," he said.

Anna paused to pick a large bouquet of lavender growing next to the stone wall.

They passed through an iron gate into an ancient churchyard. Before them lay a maze of raised tombs, many crowned with white crosses. An old woman, rosary beads draped over her right hand, bowed, then quickly left them alone. Anna noticed that some of the largest crypts had sculptures and were surrounded by photos and lit candles. In an obscure corner of the graveyard, under a large chestnut tree, Diamanté stopped in front of a crypt that was almost totally overgrown with ivy. Stone roses, surrounding the name Loupré engraved in large letters, could be seen on the front. Anna went around the back. She pulled away the dense vine to read the inscription: "*Ici repose la famille Loupré.*" Then, from left to right, were the names: Diamanté's father, Jean-Pierre Dante; his mother, Tesa; brother, Ferdinand; wife, Clotilde; and son, Diamanté *fils*.

Anna kneeled and laid the bouquet of lavender at the base of the crypt. Then she touched her father's name. As she did, she fingered the slim coin that rested on a chain in the hollow of her throat. Diamanté had wanted her to have the gold piece, which had been given to him by an advisor to the French airborne troops after the Algerian War. The coin's story, according to Diamanté, dated back to January 1962, when his son had just arrived in Algeria and the population was hoarding gold. Diamanté *fils* had saved a young Muslim boy during a massacre in which his entire family had been wiped out. The boy had given him the coin for luck. Sadly, Diamanté *fils* had met his death mere days before the cease-fire that ended the war.

Anna looked up at her grandfather and saw him discreetly wiping a tear from his cheek. She rose and went over to embrace him. "Thank you for bringing us here," she said.

***

They reached Saint-Florent late afternoon. Unlike Speloncato, the bustling waterfront town was full of tourists. Diamanté pulled up in front of a restaurant, Le Canard Corse.

Anna laughed and rolled her eyes. "Naturally," she said. "Jacques's *resto* had to be named after the bloody duck."

"*Oui, c'est ironique.*" Diamanté chuckled. "I understand he rarely serves it now."

"What's his *specialité* here?"

"*Sanglier*, wild boar. *Mais oui*," he said, anticipating her next question, "he has a boar story, too."

"I can just picture it now: a large wild pig with an apple protruding from its mouth! I hope I never have to hear that story." She looked at her grandfather. "I'm dreading seeing him, you know."

Diamanté put a reassuring hand on her arm. "Let me go in first," he said. "Take Luc for a walk around the marina." He opened the car door and glanced at the sleepy toddler in the backseat. "He'll like the sailboats. I'll signal to you when it's a good time to bring him in."

Jacques was in the restaurant kitchen noisily chopping vegetables. When he saw Diamanté, he set down the kitchen knife and grabbed a towel to wipe his hands.

"*Comu sì?*" he said in his native Corsican, wrapping massive arms around his old friend. "How are you?"

Tears welled in Diamanté's eyes as he embraced Jacques. The two men had known each other since the days of the Résistance during the Second World War.

Jacques cleared his throat. "What brings you to Saint-Florent, *mon ami?*"

"I've been to visit the cemetery in Speloncato where my family is buried," Diamanté replied.

Jacques nodded. "It is good, sometimes, to think about those who are gone. Come sit down," he added. "Let's have a *pastaga* for old times, *hein*? Just like in Marseilles." He led Diamanté into the bar and went behind the zinc.

"I've brought someone with me," Diamanté said as Jacques set a pitcher of water on the counter between them and poured two glasses of *pastis,* the anise-flavored liqueur.

"Elise?"

"*Non.* She had to stay back to run the *resto.*"

Jacques added water to his glass. The dark, transparent liquid turned a milky yellow. He raised the tumbler into the air. "*Santé,*" he said.

Diamanté returned the toast.

"*Alors, mon vieux*, who have you brought to Corsica?"

"Someone for you to meet," Diamanté said. He downed a gulp of the strong liqueur, then coughed. "Your grandson."

Chapter Sixteen

Nicko's yacht was, once again, in Bastia. Its bright lights dominated the port as I walked the short distance from my small apartment to the hospital. It was a nice evening. There were people eating at the outdoor cafés in the square, and couples dressed for clubbing. I briefly wondered where Nicko was. This was his kind of night. Just then my mobile phone rang. I answered and heard his voice.

"Time to party, Charlie," he said.

I laughed. He told me he had a new girl for me to meet. I momentarily pondered what this one would look like.

Two hours later, I was getting tired and bored and looking at my watch to see how much longer before I could leave the hospital, when I felt the beeper vibrate in my coat pocket. I was needed urgently; a possible heart attack victim was being brought in. I rushed to my station to make sure everyone was prepared. The door opened wide, and when I saw the man accompanying the patient, I recognized him in an instant: the face, furrowed with the years; the black, wolf like eyes; and the deep scar on his right temple visible under the black beret. It was unmistakably Diamanté Loupré-Tigre. My pulse raced when I realized who was on the gurney being wheeled in.

The ambulance doctor from the state-run emergency medical service SAMU (*Service d'Aide Médicale Urgente*) hollered at me, "He's unconscious. We need to administer oxygen immediately!"

Diamanté stared at me in disbelief.

"Wait here," I said to him as I followed the gurney into the room. I stood over my gravely ill father and saw clearly how the years had taken their toll on the old man. He seemed smaller and more vulnerable. His face had the deep furrows of an old piece of weathered wood, and his bulbous nose seemed to have grown even larger, the crook in it more pronounced. His thick, totally white hair had receded to give him a slightly balding look, and his eyebrows, though still black, had become even more unruly.

I quickly took his pulse and checked his vitals. He was weak, but surprisingly stable. I wondered why he was in Bastia.

"Let me know immediately if he shows signs of waking," I said to the head nurse. "I'll be just outside in the corridor with the man who brought him in."

Diamanté was nervously waiting by the door. I shook his hand warmly and took him aside.

"Charlie? It is really you?"

I smiled and nodded my head. "*Oui. C'est moi.*"

Diamanté seemed very distressed "How is he?" he asked, looking through the curtained door of my father's room.

"It's too early to say, but his signs are stable for the moment."

Diamanté was just about to tell me something when Nicko appeared. "*Salut*, Doc," he said to me, flashing a wide smile. He pushed himself between Diamanté and me. With his back to Diamanté, he offered me his hand. I was surprised by his rudeness.

"*Bonsoir*, Nicko," I said as I steered him back toward the entrance. "I'll call you later. I'm occupied just now with an emergency."

Nicko wasn't about to be dismissed. He shrugged me off, turned around, and directed his attention toward Diamanté. "Name's Manos. Nicolos Manos," he said, quickly flashing an official-looking badge in Diamanté's direction. "Hospital security."

Since when? I gave Nicko a startled, questioning look, which he ignored.

"Diamanté Loupré-Tigre."

Nicko stared at him. His gaze narrowed, and I saw a look on his face I'd never seen before.

"Loupré, you say?" He cocked his head sideways. "From the northern region?"

Diamanté seemed uneasy. He hesitated, studying Nicko's face. "Originally, *oui*," he said finally.

Nicko's nostrils flared. It was uncharacteristic for him to act this way.

I decided to intervene. "Nicko," I said sternly, "go get your girlfriend. I'll call you later." I pointed my head toward the entrance, hoping he'd get the hint to leave.

Nicko held his hands in the air and backed off. "Sorry, *mon vieux*," he said. "I'll just be over by the door, if you need me."

I gave him a look of dismay, but he appeared oblivious.

"What's with the fellow?" Diamanté said. "The *mec* doesn't look like a security guard to me."

"He's not," I whispered, scratching my head. "Of that, I'm sure. He likes to joke around a lot. He's harmless enough."

Diamanté put his hand on my shoulder. "How are you, *mon ami?*" he asked.

"*Assez bien.* As well as can be expected. I traveled for a while. Now, I have a new life here. No one knows who I really am. It is mostly okay." I stared into Diamanté's eyes. "Does my father know?" I whispered.

He shook his head. "I was told not to tell him, Charlie."

"He must have suffered terrible grief."

He nodded in agreement.

"It could have been avoided."

He nodded again. "*Désolé.* I'm sorry."

"What about Anna? How is she? Have you seen her?"

Diamanté looked at me. He smiled kindly. "Anna is fine. She's wonderful, in fact, still as beautiful, and"—he covered his mouth to stifle a slight cough, then cleared his throat and continued—"I have to tell you something, Charlie. You have a son."

I could see Nicko straining to listen from his post by the door. Stunned, I looked at Diamanté. How could I have a son? What was the old man talking about? Maybe I hadn't heard him correctly.

"What? What did you say?"

"It happened the summer of my wedding in Castagniers. You left too soon, before Anna knew."

I felt a sharp pain in the pit of my stomach. "There has to be some mistake," I said, shaking my head.

"No mistake," Diamanté replied. "The boy looks just like you. He is three now."

"What's his name?"

"Luc."

I sat down on a bench outside the door of the room where my father was lying unconscious. Nicko was talking in a low voice on his cell phone. It was as if life had suddenly come to a halt.

Diamanté seated himself on the bench beside me. "There's something else you should know," he said. "Anna is here, in Bastia, and she's brought Luc with her. We came to visit my family crypt in Speloncato and had to pass through Saint-Florent, where Jacques has his restaurant."

I was taken by surprise. "He's been living here in Corsica? All this time?"

He nodded. "Anna wanted him to know about Luc. *Merde.* I suggested we stop in to see him." He looked down at his feet and took a deep breath. "It was a terrible decision. He didn't take the news well. He wouldn't look at Luc. Anna tried to get him to understand, but he just yelled at her. Then, suddenly, he clutched his chest and..." Diamanté closed his eyes and pinched the septum of his nose.

I rested my hand sympathetically on his arm and asked, "Where is Anna now?"

"She and Luc are at a hotel not far from here, the Hôtel Central on rue Miot, just off boulevard Paoli, room six."

"Wait here," I said in a daze as I got up from the bench. "I want to see them, but first, I need to check on my father again."

Diamanté nodded. He removed his beret and rubbed the scar on his forehead. From across the waiting area, Nicko was staring at him.

Chapter Seventeen

I left my father's bedside. He was stable, breathing on his own, and sleeping peacefully. I was anxious to go with Diamanté to see Anna.

Diamanté wasn't in the corridor where I had left him. Curiously, neither was Nicko. I checked the lobby, the front steps, then returned to the desk and asked the receptionist if she had seen an elderly man in a black beret leave the hospital.

She nodded her head. "*Oui*," she said. "He was with a younger guy." She produced a grin. "Curly black hair. Handsome."

The same reaction Nicko always got.

"Did you see which direction they went?" I asked.

She pointed, smiling. "Toward the port, I think. At least they turned that way."

"*Monsieur le Docteur, venez tout de suite!*" The intensive care nurse was running toward me. She told me I needed to come immediately. The patient had awakened.

I hurried into the room and dismissed my staff, saying, "Please give me a private moment with him." I waited for them to leave and closed the door.

My father was groggy. He seemed confused about where he was. When I stepped into his line of vision, his already pale face turned white.

"*Mon Dieu*," he moaned. His voice was gravelly and strained. "There is a hereafter, *enfin*. My son and I are together again. I never believed." He suppressed a sob.

"You aren't dead," I said, embracing him. "And neither am I."

"But, but we buried you," he blubbered.

I checked the instruments monitoring him. "You didn't have a heart attack after all," I told him.

He rubbed his chest. "*Dieu, merci.*"

"It was most likely a panic attack brought on by a sudden outburst of extreme anger." I looked at him sternly. "What you need now is rest."

"But where have you been, Charlie? All this time I thought you were dead."

"It wasn't me you buried. I will tell you the whole story later. I've been living here in Bastia. I have a new identity…" I scratched my head. "No life."

He looked at me as if I were a ghost.

"I learned something today from Diamanté," I continued. I hesitated, not wanting to upset him. "Do you remember what caused the outburst of anger that landed you here?" I asked. "The visit by Diamanté and Anna?"

My father was staring at me. He remembered.

"I thought it was all a lie," he said finally, his voice raspy. "I didn't believe her. I was sure it was a scheme." He looked at me and seemed to soften, breaking into tears again. "The boy does look like you," he said between sobs.

I patted his shoulder. "Anna is here in Bastia. She followed the SAMU."

He glanced around the room and asked, "Where is Diamanté?"

"He rode with you in the SAMU," I said. "But, for the moment, he seems to have disappeared."

He looked concerned. "Diamanté? Disappeared?"

"When I went just now to find him, I was told he had exited the hospital without leaving a message."

"*Nom de Dieu*," he yelled suddenly. "I feared it might come to this." He tried to rise.

I put my hand up to stop him. "What are you talking about?"

His face was flushed, and he was extremely agitated. "He knew the risk," he said. "By returning to Corsica, especially to the northern region—"

"What are you talking about?" I interrupted.

"I warned him..." he mumbled to himself, wringing his hands and shaking his head. "Don't come back here."

I sat down on the bed. "Maybe you had better start from the beginning."

He stared at me, lost in a sea of worry. The intensive care nurse entered the room. I waved her away.

"The vendetta. It's gone on for decades," he began. "The Narbon family versus the Loupré family. Diamanté was caught up in both because his mother married a Narbon after the death of her husband, Diamanté's father, who was a Loupré. Then the younger brother born of that marriage, André, and Diamanté became half brothers. As youngsters, they fought over everything, and André was a killer. They played a deadly game. It was a common game we all played in Corsica called The Seven Turns. According to Diamanté, when André played, he would kill or maim an animal or a bird. Once he even skinned their family cat." He hesitated then took a deep breath. "That night, four years ago? When André was shot?"

I shook my head.

"He had come to kill Diamanté."

"Over what?"

"They had a long-standing conflict over Elise."

"And Diamanté had just married her," I said.

"*Beh oui!*" he said, rubbing his chest. "Although I have always thought there is more to the story—especially when André tried to kill Diamanté and was himself shot. There had always been a feud, and it was only a matter of time before they came after Diamanté to avenge André's death."

"Do you think if they have kidnapped Diamanté they will kill him?"

"Undoubtedly. He's their target"—he stopped and stared wide-eyed into space—"or quite possibly his offspring. If the Narbons have learned about Anna, she and Luc could be in great danger."

"I think I know where he might be," I said, trying to calm him. "He gave me the name of a hotel nearby where he left Anna and Luc. He is probably with them. Now that I know you are all right, I'm going to go see them."

"I'm going with you." He tried to get up.

"*Non!*" I said firmly. "You are going nowhere. You need to rest."

He gave me a look, but backed down. "Be careful, Charlie."

I checked his pulse, ordered a sedative for him, and stayed until he had fallen into a deep sleep. Then I left the stale hospital air behind and walked out the back door. The evening was crisp and cool, and the clean scent of the sea air revived me. As I made my way along the side of the building and into the narrow streets, I caught a glimpse of the port and *The Blue Amulet*, lit up like a huge floating Christmas tree.

I tried to recall the scene in the hospital when Nicko appeared. What was that about being a security guard, anyway? What was Nicko doing there? He never had come into the hospital looking for me before. None of it made any sense. If Diamanté left the hospital, he had to have a good reason. I tried to convince myself that there had to be a logical explanation for his action. Maybe he had, after all, merely gone to the hotel to be with Anna and Luc. But why did he leave with Nicko, I wondered. I dialed Nicko's cell phone on my mobile, hoping he could cast some light on this. There was no answer. I recalled my father's words and thought, *Mon Dieu. A vendetta.*

Chapter Eighteen

My heart was pounding, and I was filled with apprehension as I approached the Hôtel Central on rue Miot. It was a small hotel tucked in among darkened shops and cafés on a narrow side street just off the port. I opened the door and entered. The lobby was deserted except for a clerk, who was sitting in a chair behind the desk. He looked as if I had awakened him. I asked him directions to room six.

"Up the stairs," he pointed, yawning. "First door to the right." He raised an eyebrow and inquired if I wanted him to call *Madame* and advise her that I was coming up.

"*Non*," I told him. "I want to surprise her."

He gave me a knowing nod.

The hallway was darkened. There was a faint sliver of light coming from beneath the door of room six. I closed my eyes, sucked in a breath. "*Bon courage*," I whispered, wishing myself good luck, as I knocked softly.

The door opened slowly. I heard Anna's voice saying, "I was wondering where you've been—"

I supposed she was expecting Diamanté. Then, she saw me.

"Oh my God," she said, putting her hand to her mouth. "C-C?"

I nodded. "Can I come in?"

She opened the door wide for me to enter, then closed it. "What are you doing here in Bastia? How did you find us?"

I saw that she was unchanged, a little haggard, but still so beautiful. I wanted to take her in my arms, draw her close, and kiss her passionately, but I did not.

After clearing my throat, I said, "I have been living here in Bastia for some time. I serve in the local hospital's trauma unit."

She was standing in front of me, her arms at her sides, unemotional.

I cleared my throat again and went on. "To answer your second question, Diamanté came in with my father tonight."

"How is Jacques?" she asked, coldly staring at me.

"He will recover," I told her. "It wasn't a heart attack."

"You do know what brought it on, don't you?" She crossed her arms in front of her chest.

I nodded my head. At this point, I realized she was pissed off at both my father and me, and one could hardly blame her.

"Mama?" A small voice came from the bed, breaking the tension between us. The boy was sitting up. I stared at him. He had olive skin, curly black hair, and stunning eyes.

"Diamanté told me he's mine," I said.

She forced a smile. "Yes."

I walked over to the bed and sat down.

"Mama?" Alarmed, the boy started to cry. I was a total stranger to him.

"It's okay, dear." She rushed over to comfort him, then introduced us. "This is Luc," she said to me, and to him, "This man is"—she kissed his cheek—"someone you will want to get to know better."

The boy put his thumb in his mouth and nestled his head shyly against her neck.

"He's handsome," I said.

"He has your eyes."

"Why didn't you tell me you were pregnant when I came to California to see you, *amour*?" I called her *amour* again, "my love," just like before. If she heard it, she didn't react.

"I didn't know until after you left," she said with a heavy sigh. "You were gone. When I realized you weren't going to come back, I married Mark."

It was then that I knew I had lost her for good. She was married. I watched her cuddling Luc, and I envied Mark. I heard the sound of a car passing in the street below. In the distance, a SAMU's siren bleated.

"Mark is a lucky man," I said finally, breaking the silence.

"He's dead," she said in a voice so low it was almost a whisper.

I didn't think I'd heard her correctly. "What did you say?"

"He died in…" She stopped, then went on. "He was in New York City, in the World Trade Center, in September, when the terrorists attacked." She repressed a sob. "Luc has a beautiful little sister, Isabelle, who never saw her father."

I couldn't accurately describe the range of emotions I felt: utter anguish at her grief, and, on the other hand, elation that I had a second chance.

"I am so sorry," I said. I attempted to put my arms around her, but the toddler pushed me away angrily and burst into tears.

"I want my daddy," he wailed at the top of his lungs.

Anna rocked him gently to quiet him. "He still doesn't understand why Mark isn't with us any longer."

"Maybe I can help," I said.

"Do you really mean that, C-C?" I heard anger and frustration in her voice.

"Listen to me, Anna. I realize what you must think of me. There is something I want you to know. That day, in Castagniers, when the accident was staged? I had planned to ask you to marry me."

I could see she wasn't expecting that. She was staring at me.

"Look, I know you've been through a lot, *amour*," I went on. "Perhaps we can start over."

"How is that possible?" she responded frostily.

She was right, of course. I was a fugitive of sorts. How could we live a normal life?

Just then, I remembered Diamanté. "Your grandfather left the hospital some time ago. Do you know where he is?"

She checked her watch. "He should have been here by now. We are planning to catch the midnight ferry for Nice." She released Luc and got up. "He has his own room. I'll go knock on his door. Perhaps he's asleep."

She told Luc she'd be right back, then turned to open the door. She was wearing all black: slim pants and a tight-fitting sleeveless top that flattered her figure. Her hair was pulled back into a chignon, and, just before the door shut, I caught a glimpse of that sensuous area of her bare back I always found so irresistible.

The boy was looking at me strangely. His lips quivered, and his face was poised for another wail.

I attempted a smile, then showed him a trick. It was a simple one that I used with fearful children who came into urgent care. I made two fists and held them together, knuckles touching.

"*Voilà l'église.*" I said it first in French, then immediately realized I must use English. "A church."

He nodded.

Next, I raised my pointer fingers and touched them together. "*Le clocher*, the steeple."

He was watching me.

I opened my thumbs and wiggled my fingers. "All the people," I said.

He giggled. "I want to do it!"

Hearing his laughter, I felt a surge of warmth I had never before experienced. I wanted to protect this little boy who was my son, my own flesh and blood.

When Anna returned, Luc was happily making his own fingers wiggle. "Mama, look! People in church!" he said to her.

She smiled at me. I swiped my brow in a gesture of fake relief.

"He hasn't returned," she said. "The key is downstairs."

"I'll see you to the ferry. He may be planning to meet you there. Will you be going back to Castagniers?"

"No, to Monique's vacation home near Grasse. Isabelle is there." She quickly wrote a phone number on a sheet of hotel stationary and handed it to me. "This is my cell phone. I hope something hasn't happened to my grandfather."

I shrugged and said simply, "Corsica is a strange place, but he is a man who can take care of himself."

"I have been told that before," she said with a sigh.

Chapter Nineteen

I made my way back to the hospital as quickly as I could after seeing Anna and Luc off at the ferry landing. Her stern words resonated in my head.

"Do you remember what you said the day you left me, C-C? You told me our dance was over. I felt like you had thrust a dagger deep into my heart."

As I walked, my memory flashed back to scenes of our days in Paris together: leisurely strolls along the banks of the Seine, passionate lovemaking, waltzing to Strauss. She had lost so much. I didn't know if I could ever compensate for that, but I promised myself that I would try to make it up to her. And, I thought, how I yearned to dance with her again.

I entered my father's room and saw that he was sleeping. Diamanté was not there. I whispered to the nurse to take a break. My father heard me and opened his eyes.

"Charlie?" His normally gruff voice was uncharacteristically weak.

"Don't try to talk. Are you feeling better?"

"I feel like *merde*," he said, looking away and rubbing his chest.

"Anna and Luc have returned to Nice."

He focused one eye on me. "You saw Luc, then."

"*Oui.*"

"Do you believe he is your son?"

"*Absolument.*"

We stared at each other. Tense seconds passed. Then, finally, he muttered, "*Eh bien*, I was wrong."

I nodded. He should have been apologizing to Anna, not me.

He cleared his throat. "Was Diamanté at the hotel?"

I shook my head. "He didn't show up at the ferry landing either. Anna spotted his Fiat still parked in the lot."

"*Nom de Dieu.*"

"I thought vendettas were outlawed long ago."

"Officially, *oui*," he said. "Unofficially, *non*." The drugs I ordered were making him groggy. His speech slowed. "These things can…smolder…for…for decades."

"Do you think we should call the *flics*?" I asked him. "It seems to me that if someone has kidnapped him…"

I saw it was no use to continue the conversation. The medicine had taken effect, and he had fallen back to sleep.

I looked at him and realized for the first time what the previous four years must have been like. I had selfishly thought only about my own miserable situation all that time. I left and gave my staff orders to move him immediately to a private room in a secure area of the hospital. I told them no one was to know where he was.

Then I headed to my office. On the way, I dialed Nicko's cell phone, and, once more, he didn't answer. I left a message for him to call me. I checked my watch. It was half past midnight. I wondered where he could be.

I sat down at my desk, brought up the Internet on my PC, and checked my bank account in Nice. After transferring sufficient funds to cover the expenses for my father's hospitalization, I did a search on "André Narbon Corsica born circa 1925." André Narbon's name appeared on a website listing members of the Narbon family of Corsica. Curiously, there wasn't a date of death, only a note to the effect that an Interpol wanted (red) notice was withdrawn in 1998. I went through what sparse information there was and saw that in 1944 he married a French woman, Marie Duclos (born 1926, deceased 1947). They had two children: André *fils* (born 1945) and Anastasia (born 1947, deceased 1977).

I clicked on André Junior. In short time, I learned that he was a wealthy landowner from Calvi, on the northwest coast. His primary business was boat rental. The site showed he owned a large fleet of watercraft of various sizes. I was astonished to see a familiar name, *The Blue Amulet*, on the short list of mega-yachts at the bottom. I clicked on the link, and a photo came up showing a sleek white ship cruising on open seas. A towering satellite navigation system, its crown of jewels, extended high into the clear blue sky above the bridge. I read the description underneath.

A maritime marvel. Luxury Greek-built four-deck motor yacht sleeps fourteen in seven staterooms, plus separate quarters for the crew.
Location: Mediterranean Sea
Year Built: 2000
Length Overall: 205.0 f / 62.5 m
Beam: 38.6 ft / 11.8 m
Cruising / Max Speed: 15 / 16.8 knots

I skipped over the long list of amenities and noted with interest the communications equipment: radar, sonar, wireless and wired LAN network, GPS, autopilot, and computer charting system. I scrolled down to find a diagram and studied the six double staterooms on the lower deck. The floor plan matched that of Nicko's yacht exactly. I went back up to have another look at the photograph. It was possible, I supposed, that duplicate yachts could have been built by the same builder and given the identical name. I clicked on "lease," and a note came up:

The Blue Amulet *is currently reserved for the Narbon family's private use and is not available for charter at this time.*

There was no further information on André *fils*, so next I clicked on the daughter, Anastasia. I broke out into a cold sweat as the name Manos leapt at me from the screen.

Anastasia Narbon Manos (born 1947, deceased 1977). Married (1966) to Greek shipping magnate Alexander Demios-Manos (born 1930, deceased 1977). One son, Nicolos Narbon-Manos (born Aetopetra, Greece, 1967).

I could not believe what I was reading. Nicko? A member of the Narbon family? I clicked on his name, and a photo came up. It looked as if it had been taken a few years before, but, sure enough, there was my friend Nicko smiling at me.

Under the picture, there was only this statement:

Information restricted; written authorization required by British Secret Intelligence Service / MI6.

Chapter Twenty

Aboard *The Blue Amulet*, in a darkened starboard cabin below the first deck, Diamanté lay on a bed listening to the sounds of the yacht at night: waves lapping gently against the hull, a slight creaking with the rolling motion of the sea, a ship's horn in the distance, the barking of a lone dog in the port, echoing over the water after midnight. The air in the stateroom was stifling. He wished he could get up to open the porthole, but his hands and feet were bound.

"*Au secours! Au secours!* Help! Is anyone there?" he called out. The effort only brought on a fit of coughing.

His thoughts turned to Jacques's warning. He shouldn't have come back to the northern region, and he berated himself for not having been more vigilant at the hospital. He had carelessly left the waiting room and gone outside for a breath of fresh air. Suddenly the security guard had appeared from behind, shoved the barrel of a revolver into his ribs, and pushed him roughly through the streets of the port. When they reached a small tender docked by the pier, there was a struggle, and Diamanté had managed to grab the man's arm, causing the gun to fly into the water. In an outburst of anger, the young man had hit Diamanté with his fist, knocked him to his knees, and flung him into the small boat like a sack of potatoes. When a concerned couple passing by tried to help, they were told that Diamanté had had too much to drink.

Now, for some unexplained reason, Diamanté was being held captive on this ship. He had recognized the large yacht as the tender approached it. Anna had commented on the design on its prow just the day before. He tried to think how to escape. He had survived many horrors in his life, and had always found a way out. As a member of the Résistance during the war, he had been captured by the enemy, tortured, shot, thrown in a prison cell, and severely beaten, but he had always managed to escape. Just as he was seized by another coughing spasm, he heard someone unlocking the door.

A tall man, dressed in black jeans and T-shirt, entered the stateroom, switched on bright overhead lights, and sat down in a chair opposite the bed.

Diamanté blinked as the laser-like light pierced his eyes and made them water.

"Who are you? Why have you brought me here?" he snarled.

"Manos. Nicolos Manos. I told you my name before," the Greek said, studying the weapon he held in the palm of his hand. He smiled, pointed it at Diamanté, then set it on the table by the bed. "You will learn why you are here in good time." He moved in closer and loosened the rope tied around Diamanté's wrists.

Diamanté rubbed his arthritic hands to rid them of the numbness as he eyeballed the handgun, a German-made Walther PP. The automatic was commonly used during the war years. He owned one himself.

"Don't get any ideas, Loupré," Manos said, pulling Diamanté to a seated position.

The old man found himself squinting to get a better look at the amulet hanging from a cord around the man's neck. Its design was similar to that on the yacht's hull.

"You aren't a hospital security guard, are you?" he asked.

Ignoring him, Manos fished a packet of cigarettes from his shirt pocket.

"These are Greek. Karelias," he said as he carefully drew a slim white stick from the pack. "Do you want one?"

Diamanté shook his head.

Manos lit the cigarette with a lighter, inhaled a full breath, and exhaled. A white cloud of smoke trailed slowly toward the ceiling. With the cigarette dangling from his lips, he picked up the Walther again and ran his fingers unhurriedly over its smooth ivory handle.

Minutes passed. The only sound came from the low purr of the ship's electronics and the constant lapping of the water on the hull. The smoke made the cabin air even more unbearable, and Diamanté fought the urge to cough again. His heart beat rapidly.

The mec *is taking his time. Making me sweat,* he thought, recognizing the tactic as one guaranteed to produce terror.

"Who do you think I am?" he asked, finally breaking the silence.

Manos plucked the cigarette from his mouth and studied it indifferently. "We know who you are, Loupré," he sniffed. "You entered Corsica yesterday on the ferry from Nice. We tracked you to Speloncato. A woman and a child accompanied you when you visited Saint-Florent." He leaned forward and positioned his face directly in front of Diamanté's. "There is someone who desires to learn what happened to André Narbon, and he believes you know the answer."

Diamanté stared at him. "Who wants to know, *salaud?*" he asked in a raspy voice.

Manos curled his lip. "André never returned to Corsica. His family wishes to know what happened to him and, since they presume he is dead, where his body is. *Compris?* Do you understand?"

"I'm not the Loupré you are after," Diamanté said, shaking his head. Then, hoping to confuse the issue, he added, "My name is Loupré-Tigre." He had long ago added the *nom de guerre* of a close friend, known as *le Tigre,* killed during the war.

"*Tiens!* Really! *Eh bien*, our intelligence confirms otherwise." Manos flicked his ashes into an ashtray. "Now, *mon vieux*, answer the question. What happened to André Narbon?"

Diamanté was beginning to catch on. His half brother, a wanted terrorist and assassin, had arrived in Castagniers with the intent to kill him in August 1998. Instead, André himself had died. Had the Narbons been waiting all this time to avenge a death, or, just maybe, did they still not know exactly what happened to him? Corsican vendettas, blood feuds that erupted between families, sometimes took years to carry out. Bodies disappeared.

Diamanté spat. "André's dead," he said, looking Manos directly in the eyes. "What's it to you personally?"

Manos smiled as he played with the Walther, passing it back and forth from one hand to the other. "My mother, Anastasia, was André's daughter."

Diamanté glowered at him. "I didn't know he had a daughter." André had once mentioned casually that he had been briefly married during the war, but he had not said anything about having children. Diamanté studied the rugged structure of Manos's face, seeing no resemblance to his half brother. This man was tall and muscular. André was a small man with malicious eyes and a face like a rodent's. His *nom de guerre* during the war had been *l'Écureuil*, "the Squirrel." Was André really this man's grandfather?

"He had a son, too," Manos went on. "André Narbon *fils*, my uncle, is the owner of this yacht." Manos sat up in the chair. Then he leaned forward. His wide face again moved in close to Diamanté's. "He demands to know what happened to his father. We believe you are the one who killed him. It is time to settle the score, so to speak."

The two men glared at each other.

"Tell me. *Eh?* What happened to André Narbon?" Manos demanded again, pointing the revolver directly between Diamanté's eyes.

"*Enfin*, I told you. He is dead," Diamanté said, spitting in Manos's face. "But I didn't kill him."

Manos's nostrils flared. He raised the weapon angrily above his head.

"If not you, *qui alors?* Who then? You must know." His fierce eyes glowed like two fiery coals.

Diamanté refused to answer.

***

Gripping the pistol, Manos viciously struck Diamanté in a single violent downward motion, adding the weight of the gun to the force of the blow and using its metal frame as a point of impact.

"Let that be a lesson to you, *salaud moche*," he said angrily as the old man slumped to the floor unconscious.

I'll get him to tell me who killed Grandfather, he thought as he left the cabin. *All I have to do is find his family. That will make him talk.*

Manos turned on his cell phone as he ascended the spiral central staircase that led to the upper salon. Charlie had tried to call him several times. Well, he could wait.

"Sorry. No party tonight, *mon ami*," he said aloud.

He poured a snifter of brandy from a crystal decanter at the bar and sat down on one of the overstuffed couches. He had more important things to attend to. He needed to alert the crew. They would be underway for Calvi at dawn.

Chapter Twenty-One

Just after one o'clock in the morning, Diamanté woke to pitch darkness, his head splitting with pain. Thinking he had gone blind, he sat up quickly and touched his temple. It all came back to him: Manos, the vicious pistol-whipping. He tried to raise himself from the floor, but his head was spinning. The yacht listed slightly, causing him to fall back against the side of the bed.

"*Merde*," he spat. *I need to find a way out of here.*

He crawled on his knees around the king-size bed to the stateroom door and reached up to turn the handle. It was locked. Pulling himself to a stand, he was surprised he could see the lowered lights of the harbor through the small porthole.

Merci Dieu, he thought, relieved that he hadn't been blinded by the attack after all.

He opened the small window, allowing some welcome sea air into the stuffy cabin. As he looked out over the water, the shadow of a dinghy, moving slowly toward the yacht in the darkness, caught his attention. Intrigued that anyone could get that close without being detected, Diamanté continued to watch until it disappeared round the stern.

***

From my position in the dinghy, I scrutinized the yacht's decks. All the exterior lights had been extinguished for the night, and the bridge was dimmed. I looked to the grand salon, Nicko's party room on the upper deck, where I had been many times. Furnished lavishly, the compartment was finished in wood paneling, and had a fireplace and enough space for a baby grand piano. I could see the small twinkling lights of the crystal chandelier over the dining area, and the shadow of someone moving around.

I considered where Diamanté might be. If he was aboard, I wouldn't have much time to find him. Given the feud, there was a strong possibility the Narbons had already done away with him and disposed of the body.

Of one thing I was fairly certain. Nicko was behind Diamanté's disappearance. I could think of two probable areas on board where they might be harboring him: a small quarter berth aft, used mostly for storage, and the vacant stateroom next to mine.

I weighed both possibilities in my mind as I glided the dinghy round the stern. There were no lights, and I groped for the hooks to tie up. Then I quickly boarded the yacht. In the darkness, I edged my way along the lazarette, toward the bow, where I felt for the door of the guest stateroom for which I had a key. I unlocked it and let myself in. The cabin shared a head with the unoccupied one. I entered and saw that the door to the adjacent room was open. As I peered inside, someone grabbed me and put me in a choke hold. I couldn't breathe.

"I kill you if you make any noise, *salopard*," a man's angry voice threatened me.

Startled, I raised my hands in surrender.

"Diamanté," I whispered, "it's Charlie. I came to get you out of here."

Diamanté dropped his hold on me.

"My ankles are bound," he said.

I bent and quickly cut the rope with the Swiss Army knife I always carried with me.

I led Diamanté into the adjoining cabin. We waited, listening in the dark. I could hear my own heart beating. Diamanté was so quiet I wondered if he was even behind me. Sneaking into the corridor, he followed me noiselessly as we inched past the lazarette. I was just about to untie the dinghy when the yacht's bright arc searchlights flashed on in unison. A spotlight was trained on us, and we heard men's voices. A figure leaned over the upper deck and aimed an assault rifle directly at us.

"Jump," I yelled.

The two of us dived overboard. I heard the *thrup thrup thrup* of bullets hitting the water's surface. I swam underwater along the hull until I reached the bow, then raised myself just enough to gulp some air. I didn't see Diamanté anywhere. Panicking, I realized I needed to find him. I edged my way aft. Amidships, I collided with a body totally submerged and struggling. It was Diamanté. I grabbed hold of his collar, and it took all my strength to pull him back toward the bow and push his head out of the water. He came up gasping for breath and vomiting.

As the bright beam of a searchlight moved slowly across the surface, closing in on us, I asked him, "Can you swim?"

"I'm hit…in the leg. I don't have any feeling."

"Grab my shoulders and hang on."

Diamanté nodded, took in a deep breath, and put his arms firmly around my neck.

Towing Diamanté with me, I could not keep my head above water. I swam along the hull, pushing myself until my lungs were nearly ready to burst. I had never been a strong swimmer, but fear seemed to have produced extra adrenalin. My arms ached, and I was unsure how long either of us could last. Diamanté had not passed out since he was still clinging to me. We finally surfaced, both of us gasping for air, out of the beam of the yacht's searchlight and on the port side.

I could tell Diamanté was weakening, as he was barely able to keep his head above water. I didn't know how much longer I could go on towing him, either. Just then, I spotted a small fishing boat coming toward us. As the trawler neared, I raised my right arm and waved frantically.

***

With his assault rifle in one hand, Manos rushed to the stateroom where he had held Diamanté captive. He quickly unlocked and opened the door, and, seeing the empty room, he exploded in anger. Someone had helped Diamanté escape. But who?

Back on deck, he ran crazily fore and aft trying to locate the two men in the dark, murky water. The dinghy was still moored to the stern, but it was sinking from the bullet holes he had pumped into it. Where could they be? Had he hit them? He wondered again who the man was who had tied the mysterious inflatable to the yacht. Were others waiting nearby to pick them up? Manos scanned the surface beyond the range of the searchlights, but it was too dark. He ran up the stairs to the bridge to get his night vision goggles.

"*Qu'est-ce qui s'est passé?*" he snapped at the yacht's chief electronics engineer as he angrily threw open the door. "What happened? We had an intruder. Why wasn't the radar on?"

The man, Salim, looked up sleepily and tossed his open hands in the air. "You told me tonight was your party night, Nicko. We left the security off for your friends to board."

"I ordered the crew to be underway by morning. The ship's lights were off, you stupid fool," Manos hissed as he grabbed the infrared binoculars and stormed out of the cabin, spewing expletives in every language he knew.

***

"*Ça m'est égale,*" Salim said with a sneer as the door closed. "It's all the same to me." He shrugged his shoulders and went back to his computer screen.

Salim had worked for the Narbon family for a long time. He'd known the indulged nephew of the yacht's owner since he was a teenager. Nicko's lifestyle irritated him, and he rarely talked to him, although he did report on his activities from time to time. Tonight was one of those nights he would recount. Nicko had brought someone aboard and ordered the crew to prepare to head out two days early. It had seemed strange to him, out of character. If anything, Nicko delayed departures for a day or two to party.

Salim's primary job was to monitor the complex electronics aboard the yacht. His life centered around the intricate communications and GPS software he controlled and the bank of radar and sonar screens flashing in front of him. He rarely left his corner of the bridge, and he never took leave to visit a port. When he wasn't dozing in his chair, the dwarfish figure with his head wrapped in a peaked turban took short naps on a cot nearby. A devout Muslim, the only break he took was for his ritual prayer routine, five times daily.

"He's taking the tender," the captain hollered from the control station.

"At this time of night?" Salim answered. "What's up with the *gars*, *hein?*"

The captain shrugged. "*Sais pas.* No idea. Better track him on the radar. We'll need to record this entire incident in the ship's log."

Chapter Twenty-Two

A woman spotted us from the helm of the fishing vessel. "*Attento!*" I saw her pointing to us and hollering, "Look over there. In the water."

A man ran along the deck and threw a rope from the bow. With all the strength I could muster, I tied it around Diamanté's waist, then signaled to pull us in. Holding Diamanté to keep his head above water, I myself was almost the entire time submerged until, finally, we were lifted onto the working deck amidships.

I shielded my eyes as the woman standing over us aimed a bright beam of light directly into our faces.

"*Meu deus! Sua cara,*" the woman gasped in horror when she saw Diamanté's swollen eyes and the bruises and cuts on his forehead, cheeks, and jaw. I noted them, too, for the first time.

The man helped me to my feet. "*Mon Dieu.* Turn off lantern, Avelina," he ordered.

The woman switched off the light and backed away.

"*Qu'est-ce qui se passe?* What is going on here? Who are you?" she asked.

Behind her, I spotted three young children peering at us from the bridge. This small fishing trawler was obviously a family operation.

The man shook my hand, then Diamanté's, and introduced himself. "*Mon nom* Odoardo," he said in heavily accented French. "*Meus apologies, messieurs.* My wife, Avelina, she afraid. We simple *pescadors*, from Portugal *originalmente*." He pulled a long-stemmed smoking pipe from his jacket pocket and tapped it into the palm of his hand. "We normally not fish humans out of water," he said, muffling a chuckle. He watched us as he held a burner lighter skillfully over the hand-carved meerschaum. There was a quick flash, and the scent of sweet tobacco smoke filled the air.

"I am a doctor," I said. "This man has been shot. Can you help us?"

The man and wife looked at each other, wide-eyed. "Shot?" they said in unison.

"In the leg," Diamanté said. His voice was very weak, and he was trembling. "It was an accident. We are not criminals, *mon ami*. We only ask a simple favor. Can you take us back to port?"

"*Impossível!* Impossible," the woman said, pulling her husband back. "We are just headed out of the harbor."

"These men need help, *caro*," Odoardo said, patting his wife's arm. "*Por favor.* Return to wheelhouse."

Avelina raised her shoulders in disgust, then turned on her heel and headed back to the bridge and her wide-eyed children.

"*Bom então.* We go inside," Odoardo said to me. Together, we carried Diamanté into a small cabin and laid him on a cot. In the dim light, I was able to examine Diamanté's bullet wound.

"You were lucky," I said after a few minutes. "It appears to have gone completely through. Bounced off the femur and exited the other side. See here?"

"Will I be able to walk again?" he asked, suddenly overcome by a rattling cough emanating from deep in his chest.

"There is some damage to the leg. We'll need to get you to a hospital," I said, concerned that he might also be developing pneumonia.

Odoardo was standing by the doorway, smoking his pipe and watching us with suspicion.

"Could you possibly take us to Nice, *monsieur*?" I asked him. "I'll make it worth your while. Whatever the cost, the loss of your day's take, I can pay."

Odoardo drew a deep pull and let the smoke slowly release through his nostrils. He looked out at the open sea, then down at his feet. Finally, he said, spitting a piece of tobacco from his tongue, "I talk about it with my wife." He left, and we heard a heated discussion neither of us could understand because it was in Portuguese, but it went on for some time.

While we waited for the verdict, I set about bandaging Diamanté's wounded leg and treating the cuts and bruises on his head and face with first aid supplies delivered by one of the children, a boy of about eleven.

Avelina entered alone some time later. She had pulled a heavy shawl over her head and shoulders to shield her from the cold sea air. I noted that her face was weathered, but she appeared to be no older than thirty-five.

She gave Diamanté a stern look. "I am reluctant," she began, clearing her throat, "but Odoardo insists we should help you. We will take you to Nice. The journey will be several hours."

She was evidently the most fluent in French of the two, and I heard only a faint accent.

"How many hours?" I asked.

"This boat only does eleven knots at its fastest. Depending on the sea, it will be at least ten hours to Nice. Do you think he can make it?" She gave Diamanté a sideways glance.

I nodded. "We would be very grateful, *madame*."

"*Bom.*" She cleared her throat again. "One more piece of business, then, *monsieur*. The cost of the voyage will be twelve thousand euros. With the loss of at least two days' catch, you know." She shrugged her shoulders and tightened her lips. "And then there's the extra expense for fuel and supplies for feeding two more."

I considered her statements thoughtfully. "I understand the hardship, *madame*, on you and your family. I am in no position to bargain, *bien sûr*, but I would be happy if you would accept ten thousand euros in return for your hospitality."

The woman stood firmly in her place, a frown on her face, her arms crossed in front of her chest. "*Bom*. Considering the circumstances in which you find yourselves on our vessel, the gunshot wound sustained by one of you, and the unknown danger to our family, we will provide you with our 'hospitality,' as you say, for eleven thousand euros. No less."

Diamanté had thankfully fallen asleep on the cot.

"Let's get underway," I said. "You will get your money when we arrive in Nice."

"Very well, then," said she with a determined look. "I will have my son, Christophe, deliver some dry clothing and blankets to you." With that, she marched off to the helm.

We moved swiftly away from the harbor. I went out on the deck and stared at *The Blue Amulet* in the distance, its bright spotlights still searching the surface of the water. I hoped no one suspected we were on this fishing boat. The fast-moving yacht could have easily overtaken the small vessel in no time. I was putting this family in a great deal of danger, but I had no choice.

***

As we made our way into the Mediterranean Sea en route to mainland France, I heard a series of explosions. In the dark, I smiled to myself. The sky over Bastia harbor was aglow in red.

Chapter Twenty-Three

In Bastia harbor, moonlight glistened on the water's surface, and vessels of all types and sizes, their lights low, bobbed and swayed gently in sync with the peaceful summer breeze coming off the sea.

Enraged at Diamanté's bold escape, Manos slowly maneuvered the tender along *The Blue Amulet*'s hull. Like a predator hunting his prey, he stared intently through his night vision goggles as he encircled the yacht. Seeing nothing, he turned, wild-eyed, in the direction of the port, veering at the last minute out of the way of a fishing trawler that was headed straight toward him.

In the marina, Manos tied up the small boat and stood on the quay with his hands on his hips. He surveyed the tall, faded buildings and the deserted streets of the old port and wondered how he was going to locate Diamanté. Where could he have gone?

Suddenly, Manos felt the concussion of a huge explosion behind his back. The quay rocked, and the blast shattered windows in the port. He turned, and his heart leapt into his throat as he stared in horror at *The Blue Amulet*, flames shooting from its hold, and dense black smoke pouring from the sleek aluminum hull. Realizing that he had taken the craft's only lifeboat, he quickly jumped into the tender, put the motor on full speed, and raced toward the conflagration. Harbor police and fireboats arrived. A helicopter appeared from nowhere and circled over the scene. Loudspeakers warned all to stay back at a safe distance. It was futile to try to get any closer.

Manos sat in the gently rocking tender, seething with anger and feeling helpless. He'd been set up by Diamanté, he concluded. The scheming old man had lined up his accomplices and waited for the moment when the *Amulet*'s crew let down their guard. But who had helped him? Moreover, where were they now?

"*Skata*," he swore in Greek under his breath. His uncle would be furious. Not to mention the Sicilian owner of the undelivered cargo of munitions they had picked up in Marseilles earlier in the week. He would have a lot of explaining to do, especially when it was discovered that members of the crew had no lifeboat in which to escape.

Diamanté Loupré had destroyed his world.

Another blast rocked the *Amulet*. As sparks rained down on him, Manos shook his fist in the air.

"You will pay for this night, *katheki*," he yelled.

From now on, his only focus would be deadly retaliation against Diamanté and his family.

CHAPTER TWENTY-FOUR

Castagniers, France

The last of the Ajaccio's guests had gone upstairs. A weary Elise bid the sous-chef *bonne nuit,* turned out the kitchen lights, and climbed the flight of steps to the salon. She looked at her watch with a sigh. It was nearing two o'clock. The day had been demanding, and she had to be up at six to prepare for the morning breakfast service. It was a good thing they had hired extra help for the month of August, she thought, especially now that she was having to run things all by herself for a few days.

In the library, the large flat-screen TV was still on, and a lone guest, Mr. Muranaka, was watching a late-night news broadcast. Elise greeted him and, exhausted, plopped herself into an easy chair. The Japanese man bowed his head, then nodded toward the television. *FLASH INFO* in red letters raced across the screen. The scene, shot from a news helicopter, showed smoke pouring from the stern of a large yacht. Underneath, the banner read: *Live from Bastia, Corsica.*

Elise gulped and sat up.

"We have very little information at this point," the news anchor was saying. "Our sources tell us the mega-yacht has been anchored in the port for the past few days. According to an eyewitness, there seemed to be a lot of activity on the deck, and searchlights scanning the surrounding water tonight, just before a series of explosions."

Another live view from the helicopter circling the scene showed a huge plume of black smoke rising into the air above the harbor. As they watched, an explosion rocked the yacht, and flames shot from the hold like fireworks.

"As you can see," the anchor interjected, "the luxury vessel is now fully engulfed and listing badly. It doesn't look as if it will be salvageable."

The program continued with other news and then flashed back to the port of Bastia. "More on that fire off Corsica," the newscaster said as the camera panned in to show the large craft, now two-thirds submerged. "Its name is, ironically, *The Blue Amulet*. We have just received confirmation that it is EU registered and owned by a wealthy landowner from Calvi. There is suspicion explosives of some kind were on board, and it is unknown at this time whether this incident is related to recent terrorist threats made against Haute-Corse by the Fronte di Liberazione Naziunale Corsu. The FLNC, as far as we know, has not claimed responsibility for the attack. Investigators are making their way to the scene. We will keep you posted as to further developments."

"*Oh là!*" Elise exclaimed. She couldn't help wondering if Diamanté was somehow involved.

Chapter Twenty-Five

I was soaked to the bone, and the chilly night air made me shiver. As the lights of Corsica retreated into the distance, I stood on the deck listening to the steady drone of the fishing vessel's engine and took in the competing scents of salt sea air, diesel fumes, and the *maquis*. Even out that far, one could smell it. A groan came from the cabin. I went back in quickly. Diamanté had awakened.

"Are you alive?" I asked.

He chuckled and said, "Barely. My head hurts. The *mec* beat me up pretty good." With great difficulty, he pulled himself to a seated position.

"Was it Nicko?"

He nodded.

"But why? What did he want?"

"Information," he replied. "I spit in his face."

He was staring at me with one eye. In the low light of the lantern, I could see that the other was swollen shut. I examined the skeletal bone around his eye socket while I brought him up to date on my father's condition. He was relieved at the news. Then he asked how I knew to look for him on *The Blue Amulet*.

"My father told me some about the vendetta," I said. "I decided to do a quick search on the Internet to see if I could find out anything useful. When I discovered Nicko was a member of the Narbon family, I guessed where you might be. I had been on that yacht a few times. I knew the layout. Turns out I was right." I hesitated, then continued. "I have to warn you, though. There may be further retaliation. I lit my cigarette lighter and threw it in the lazarette as we were escaping, hoping it would set something on fire and create a diversion. Nicko keeps a lot of fireworks for his parties in there. I heard an explosion just after we quit the harbor."

"*Ah bon?*" he said, then exclaimed, "*Extraordinaire, alors!*"

I asked him what happened after he left the hospital.

"Nicko, as you call him, forced me into a tender at gunpoint. I tried to fight him, but he was stronger."

He winced as he tried to move his leg to a more comfortable position.

I searched the boat's small first aid kit for something to ease his pain. "There's only aspirin," I said. "Because of the danger of bleeding, we can't risk it."

The boy, Christophe, arrived with blankets and a pile of dry clothing. He left and returned with a tray of fried fish and potatoes, a crusty baguette, and two bottles of Sagres, a Portuguese beer. The food smelled wonderful. I thanked him.

I helped Diamanté pull a heavy woolen sweater over his head, then I changed into dry clothing, and both of us devoured the food and drank the beer.

"*Eh bien.* I'm proud of you, Charlie," Diamanté said suddenly. "You did well tonight."

A compliment coming from the old man.

"What limited military training I received came in handy," I said with a chuckle. "Besides, I have a reason to live, now. I have a son."

I told him about seeing Anna and Luc off to the ferry and how worried she was about him.

With a sigh, he lay back on the cot, and I heard his raspy voice. *"Eh bien, mon ami, tu m'as sauvé la vie cette nuit."*

Hearing his words, *"You saved my life tonight,"* it hit me what we had just been through together. I looked at the empty food trays and the blankets and dry clothing the fisherman and his wife had provided. I thought of Anna and Luc and felt alive. I had so much to live for. I lay down on the other cot, pulled a blanket over me, and was rocked to sleep by the sea. It would be several more hours before we reached the coast of Southern France.

***

When I awakened, it was just daybreak, and a briny smell filled my nostrils. Hearing the *Chee! Chee! Chee!* of seagulls, I realized with relief we were approaching land. I pulled myself up and quietly left the cabin.

The morning was glorious. I leaned over the railing to get a better look at the vessel. It was brightly painted in blue, gold, and white horizontal stripes. The name *Sesimbra* adorned its hull. I studied the fishing gear and watched a white pelican patiently perched on the bridge above me, his giant beak poised to scoop up breakfast.

Odoardo was working with a strange-looking wooden-and-rope mesh trap at the stern. In his orange hooded waterproof gear and black rubber boots, the long-stemmed meerschaum hanging from his mouth, he reminded me of a wood carving of a fisherman I once saw in Asia. I went over to watch him. When he saw me, he pulled off his heavy gloves and removed the pipe from his mouth.

"*Bom-dia. Bonjour*," he said cheerfully, extending his hand. "How your patient?"

"As well as can be expected," I said. "What do you catch?"

"*Lagosta*," he replied with a proud smile. "*Langouste. Sesimbra* specialty."

"Ah, spiny lobster," I said, noting the mild, crisp, clean smell in the air. "And who or what is the *Sesimbra* named for?"

"Is village in Portugal. We buy this old boat long time ago, Avelina *et moi*, and name it after our home."

"Did you paint it yourself?"

"*Sim.*" The man nodded. He appeared pleased that I was interested. "In traditional colors of Portuguese."

"It is very handsome," I said sincerely. "How much longer before we arrive in port?"

He gazed at the horizon. "*Bientôt*. Soon. Maybe two hours."

I thanked him for his hospitality and returned to the small cabin to find Diamanté snoring loudly. I listened with growing concern to the rattle in his chest and the tight, restricted breathing. An hour later, he awakened.

"You're no worse for all that's happened," I said as I checked his pulse. "You just look terrible."

He laughed.

The boy, Christophe, arrived with steaming bowls of *café crème*, a plate of warm sliced Portuguese linguica smoked sausage, and a basket of thick slices of crusty bread slathered with sweet butter and apricot preserves.

While we ate, we discussed what we would do after the *Sesimbra* docked in Nice.

Chapter Twenty-Six

As the boat pulled into the harbor, I explained to Avelina that I would leave Diamanté aboard while I called for an ambulance and, I emphasized, went to my bank so I could pay them their money for the trip. At first, she set her jaw, and I thought *Oh no, she is going to protest*, but then she waggled her head from side to side and abruptly agreed to the arrangement.

"It wasn't too bad, the crossing," she admitted. "*En effet*, as a matter of fact, we made pretty good time, and the pots we set on the way should be full, too." I thought I saw the hint of a smile in her eyes.

After thanking her for their genuine hospitality, I left the vessel and immediately purchased a replacement for my water-logged mobile phone. With it, I arranged for a SAMU to pick up Diamanté, then dialed Monique and Georges's number.

"*Allô?*" Monique answered.

I identified myself, then quickly added, "*Désolé*, Monique. I'm sorry to bother you, but I need to speak with Anna. Is she there?"

"*Oui*," she said coldly. "*Mais elle est occupée.*"

"This is urgent. It's about her grandfather."

"*Attendez*," she said curtly.

I waited. There was some discussion in the background, which I could not make out.

"C-C?" Anna was on the phone. "Where are you? Did you find *Grand-père*?"

"*Oui*," I said, hesitantly. "*C'est un peu compliqué*. A bit complicated. We are in Nice. He has been injured."

I heard her gasp. "Will he be all right?"

"A leg wound. He'll be okay." I didn't mention that we were going to the hospital.

"But how? Why? What happened?"

There was no time to explain all that had transpired during the past few hours, so I decided to merely tell her that he had been in an accident and that was why he had missed the ferry.

She asked if we'd notified Elise.

"*Non*," I said. "We just got in. Could you call her? It would be better, I think. Reassure her we will be in Castagniers as soon as we can."

"She's been wanting to see Isabelle. Maybe I'll drive over with the children this afternoon. How can we reach you?"

I gave her the number of my mobile.

"Please tell *Grand-père* I love him," she said.

"*Bien sûr*," I said, adding, "by the way, can you ask Elise if they saved any of my clothing when they cleared out the house? Unfortunately, I look like a Portuguese *pescador* right now. I even have the beginning of a beard to match."

Anna laughed. "I can't wait to see that."

I relaxed. Just hearing her voice had relieved my tension.

***

I left the bank and heard the wail of sirens. Just as I reached the dock, the ambulance pulled up. I immediately explained about Diamanté's leg wound, being careful to describe it as an accident so as not to raise suspicion and a call to the *flics*. Then, I led the medics to the boat. While they were loading Diamanté onto a stretcher, I handed Avelina a cash-filled envelope and bid the family farewell.

From the SAMU, Diamanté and I watched the *Sesimbra* pull up anchor and leave its mooring. Odoardo and the children waved to us. At the helm, Avelina was grinning.

Diamanté chuckled. "They won't have to worry about money for a while."

The SAMU's doctor examined Diamanté's facial wounds, then began to remove the bandages from his leg. I knew he was wondering what happened, but he didn't ask. "Looks pretty clean," he said. "We've a bit of stitching up to do, but it shouldn't be necessary to keep you overnight."

Diamanté heaved a sigh of relief.

We arrived at the hospital emergency entrance, and I was suddenly reminded of my father. I dialed Centro in Bastia and was forwarded to my assistant. When she picked up, I asked if my patient had been moved to a private room.

"*Oui*, as you requested, *mais*..." She hesitated. "It's been pretty busy around here with all the excitement in the harbor."

"What excitement?" I asked casually.

"A big explosion and fire. A large yacht. You know the one. *The Blue Amulet*. It was apparently loaded with ammunition that blew up. Terrible scene. They're still searching for survivors. One burn victim has been brought in. He's in pretty bad shape."

"Has he been identified?" I asked, wondering if it could be Nicko.

"Not yet. Smallish man with a head wrap of some sort. It apparently saved his life. Oh, I forgot. Your patient? The one we had moved?"

"*Oui*. I'd like to speak with him."

"*Désolé*. He is no longer with us."

"What?"

"He just vanished. No explanation. The receptionist in the lobby said there was an inquiry earlier about him. A guy came in and flashed a badge at her. Then, when she wouldn't tell him anything, he tried to get her to go with him to have a drink." She laughed. "He swore at her and left *illico presto* when she phoned hospital security."

When I hung up, I noticed my hand was shaking.

"*The Blue Amulet* was destroyed," I told Diamanté. "Nicko apparently escaped, and my father has disappeared."

Chapter Twenty-Seven

The day was warm and sunny, and the scent of lavender filled Anna's nostrils as she drove the winding route to Castagniers.

Luc said from the backseat, "I like this place, Mama."

"Me, too, darling."

In fact, she did like it. Once she had thought it claustrophobic, but today, as they entered the small village, she had to admit how charmed she felt.

The central square was filled with tourists visiting the weekly market where local artisans had set up booths to sell their wares. As Anna got out of the car, she spotted the familiar face of the town potter, middle-aged, with a balding head and scruffy red beard, his olive skin tanned like a piece of shoe leather, and large hands caked with clay from working the potting wheel. She remembered vividly the day she had haggled with him to purchase one of his pieces. The large contemporary pitcher with its bold dark blue pattern now sat on the counter in Monique's kitchen at Beausoleil. She had probably paid too much for it, she thought now, as she waved to him. He smiled and pointed to the items on the table in front of him, then waved his hand in invitation for her to come have a look. She laughed and nodded her head. Maybe later.

Luc ran into the Ajaccio to find Max. Anna followed with Isabelle in her stroller. They found the dog sound asleep on the cool tile floor next to the zinc bar.

"Be gentle, Luc," Anna warned.

The little boy squatted and patted the soft nose with his hand. Max yawned, then rose slowly and greeted him with multiple licks on the cheek.

The headwaiter pointed her to the back patio off the kitchen, where Elise was seated on a chaise lounge. Her arm rested over her forehead, and her eyes were closed.

"Elise?" Anna whispered.

"*Oh là.* Anna."

Anna bent down and kissed her on both cheeks. "How are you?"

"*Épuisé.* Exhausted. I was just taking a break before checking in the new guests."

Anna moved the stroller closer. "I've brought the baby to meet you."

Elise rose from her seat. "*Oh là.*" She clapped her hands together in delight and wrinkled her nose in her characteristic smile. "Can I hold her?"

"*Bien sûr,*" Anna said. She gathered Isabelle into her arms and handed her to Elise just as Luc came onto the patio.

"*Oh là! Le petit chou! Bonjour!*" Elise said as she kissed the top of his head.

"What she say? Shoe?" Luc looked down at his feet.

Anna laughed. How to explain to a toddler that the French call children little cabbage heads? "She says you're sweet, dear," she finally said.

With Isabelle in her arms, Elise, her fatigue suddenly forgotten, took Luc by the hand and proceeded to show the two children off to the guests seated under the umbrellas on the terrace, then to the merchants in the marketplace, and finally to some locals playing a game of *pétanque* on a sandy lot in the park under some shade trees.

Anna followed them, amazed.

"I want food," Luc said when they had returned to the restaurant's terrace.

"Would you like a croissant, *mon petit?*" Elise chirped as she handed Isabelle to Anna. Luc nodded.

Elise seated them at an outdoor table under a large green umbrella and beckoned to the headwaiter. "Bring a basket of *croissants au chocolat*," she said. "Now I've really got to check in those guests, Anna, so if you'll excuse me…"

"Elise, I've come to tell you some news about *Grand-père*," Anna blurted out.

Elise halted, a look of alarm on her face. "I've been so worried. He didn't come back on the ferry with you, did he?"

Anna shook her head. "I received a call midday from Charlie…"

"Mon Dieu," Elise cried out. She sat down.

Anna explained about the ambulance and Jacques being taken to the hospital in Bastia where, by pure coincidence, Charlie was working in the emergency room.

"And now he's bringing Diamanté back to Castagniers," she said.

"*Oh là*, Anna. He's injured, isn't he, my Lobo?"

Anna stared at the old woman. "Yes, Elise, *Grand-père* has apparently been in some sort of accident."

"I knew it. The explosion in Bastia harbor. I just knew he was involved. I felt it." Then, suddenly, Elise gave up a huge sob.

Her comment took Anna by surprise. How could the woman have arrived at such a conclusion? She had seen the news report, too, but never in the slightest stretch of the imagination could she have thought her grandfather involved.

"Charlie said he is going to be all right."

"But where is he now? Why hasn't he called?"

"They arrived in Nice a couple of hours ago. They should be here soon."

Isabelle began to cry. Anna plucked a bottle of formula from her bag.

Just then, the Ajaccio's sous-chef came onto the patio. "*Excusez, mesdames,*" he said. "Sorry for the interruption, but there is a phone call for you, Elise. It's your husband."

"*Oh là!*" Elise wiped a tear from her eye as she hurried into the bar to take the call.

***

Anna was feeding Isabelle her bottle when Elise returned.

"*Dieu merci,*" Elise said, making the sign of the cross across her forehead. "My Lobo is on his way home."

"How is he?" Anna asked, concerned.

"He seemed very tired." Elise looked at the baby and gently patted her head. "Come. Let's take the children to the house. You'll be more comfortable there while we wait."

***

The two-story house with terra-cotta-tiled roof and sun-drenched yellow façade sat on the outskirts of the village. Elise held Luc's hand, and Anna walked behind them with Isabelle in her arms. Max, the old dog, lumbered along after them. The exterior of the house was just as Anna had remembered: light sage-green shutters, wooden gate, the front garden pathway lined by red roses and lavender. Anna took a deep breath as Elise opened the carved wooden door.

What had once served as the outer waiting room for C-C's stark medical clinic was now a stunning foyer, its floor covered in Spanish tiles. A crystal chandelier hung elegantly from the ceiling, and a huge bouquet of blue hydrangeas and yellow roses adorned an antique round mahogany table in the center.

"We've done a lot of work inside. *Enfin*, Charlie's efforts inspired us to continue."

"It's beautiful," Anna remarked as they entered an attractively furnished salon. Luc ran to one of two brocaded, overstuffed Louis XV chairs and plopped himself down.

"Where TV, Mama?" he asked, leaning back into the pillows and stretching his legs.

"I'm afraid we don't have a *télé, mon petit*," Elise responded, lifting her shoulders apologetically.

"Is Clo still here?" Anna asked.

"*Mais, bien sûr.* Of course, and he will be happy to see you," Elise answered. "Come, *petit*," she said as she grabbed Luc's hands and pulled him from the chair. "Let's go see if we can find Clo in the rose garden."

"Okay," said Luc reluctantly.

Anna smiled at him. "Clo's house looks just like it could be in Disneyland, Luc."

"It does?" The little boy's eyes opened wide. "I want to see it! Where is it?"

"It's in the garden," Anna said, remembering the first time she had looked out from the kitchen toward the quaint two-story building with a single French door, mansard roof, and window boxes full of salmon-pink geraniums. C-C had explained that his Cambodian caretaker, Clo, lived in it.

They filed through the large, low-ceilinged kitchen, past a big wooden table that sat under the light of an antique copper chandelier coated with a greenish-blue patina.

"It's such a beautiful kitchen, Elise," Anna said, recalling how she had admired the glossy *aubergine mi-professionnel* La Cornue stove and the intricate detail in the antique tiles above the gray marble work counter. "*Mais*," she sighed, "it still looks unused."

Elise clucked her tongue and shrugged her shoulders. "*Oh là. Bien sûr*, we are always at the Ajaccio for meals."

"It's such a shame. It seems like a kitchen one would love to spend time in."

"Do you like cooking, Anna?"

"Well, yes, actually."

"Then you are welcome to *inaugurer* this *cuisine*, if you wish," Elise said with a laugh.

"Let's make hot dogs, Mama," Luc said jumping up and down.

"Hot dogs?" Elise feigned shock. "*Oh là!* You eat dogs, *petit?*"

Anna laughed. "*Les sausissons*, Elise," she explained. "In a long bun. American children love them."

"*Ah oui. Les hot-dogs.*" Elise winked, and her head bobbled up and down. "I tried one on the Champs-Elysées in Paris once. It was delicious."

Anna nodded. "I had one of those, also. Best hot dog I ever ate. It was in a crunchy baguette and slathered with spicy hot mustard." Just then, she spotted the Cambodian gardener limping across the grass toward them.

"*Bonjour*, Clo," she called to him, waving.

Clo flashed a shy smile at Anna and bowed low in greeting. "You want see the roses, *madame?*" he said, pointing to the garden in full bloom.

"Of course I want to see them, Clo," Anna said eagerly as she handed the baby to Elise. Luc was already running down the small pathway toward a birdbath and bench under a white-rose arbor.

"Clo," Elise called after them, "did you bring one of the portable cribs from the Ajaccio...*pour le bébé?*"

"*Oui, madame,*" Clo said, bowing. "Just as you say. I put in big guest room. Toys, too, *pour le petit.*"

"*Bon, merci,* Clo," Elise said as she turned to go into the house. "I'll show Isabelle her new bed. Come see the upstairs when you are finished, Anna. It's complete now and entirely different. The big guest room will be perfect for you and the babies tonight."

Luc came bounding back. "Look, Mama, what Clo gave me." He held out a single rose, its color creamy ivory tinged with pink apricot. Anna bent down and scooped him into her arms. "He said it's an Anna rose, Mama. That's your name. It's your rose."

"Yes, it is," she said. The scent of the flower filled her nostrils, carrying her back to the day in August 1998 when Luc's father, C-C, had brought her a blossom from the very same bush. They had made love with abandon. Was that the day she had conceived, she wondered.

***

Three hours later, Anna sat with Isabelle in her arms on the back terrace. The scent of roses from the garden filled the soft, cool air, and a chorus of croaking frogs had begun their evening concert. In the distance, she could hear the small village band warming up in the square.

Anna's thoughts were deluged suddenly with fear, uncertainty, doubt, and guilt. When worries flooded in on her, keeping her awake at night, she had given them categories. Fear was reserved mostly for her children. Uncertainty almost always entailed her future. Doubt covered just about everything else, except the special category she had labeled Guilt. She should have gone to France with Mark. Maybe he wouldn't have departed so soon for New York. Or, if he had, maybe...just maybe, he wouldn't have died. As always, that day in September (was it only eleven months ago?), when she realized she had lost Mark forever, haunted her. What must he have gone through? She had occasionally allowed herself to imagine the unimaginable, but the pain had always become too great, and she had had to make herself dismiss the thoughts. She would never know for certain whether he had been killed instantly or had suffered a horrible death. A tear spilled down her cheek and landed on the baby's blanket. She nestled her face in the soft sleeping bundle and listened to the gentle breathing. What was she going to do with her life? She had the responsibilities of motherhood and the house in California. Then there was her writing, which she hadn't touched in months. What was next? She was still young. She had been surprised seeing C-C again. Something in her that she hadn't felt in a long while had stirred, a frisson of sexual desire. Was that all it was? She was young, still had those yearnings. She longed for male companionship. Could she ever commit to another marriage? Was it too soon to think about that?

A sudden giggle from Luc, who was playing on the grass below the steps, brought her out of her reverie.

"Look, Mama," he said as he held up a toy truck Clo had brought for him to play with.

Just then, she heard a car drive up to the garage at the back corner of the garden. She stood up, put Isabelle on her shoulder, and with Luc holding on to her skirt, the trio went down the small, darkened pathway to investigate. A black Mercedes was parked in the driveway with its headlights on.

Chapter Twenty-Eight

I opened the door and got out of the car, my throat tight at the sight of Anna and her children as they squinted at us in the light of the car's headlamps.

"How are you, C-C?" she asked nervously.

Luc tugged at her skirt.

"Mama? I'm scared, Mama."

I bent down and attempted to hug the boy, but he resisted me and began to cry.

"It's okay, sweetheart." Anna patted his head then said to me, "You *are* somewhat intimidating with that beard and in those fisherman's clothes."

I inspected myself. "I suppose I am," I said with a grin.

The passenger door of the Mercedes opened, but Diamanté did not get out. Anna gave me a look of concern.

"Your *grand-père* is a survivor," I said, "but I have to warn you. He's not the most handsome sight at the moment, and his leg is giving him a lot of pain. It will be a while before he is healed."

"Does Elise know you're here? She went back to the *resto*, but she's been very worried."

"We called her. She should arrive any minute."

"Come on," Anna said, grabbing Luc's hand. "Let's go see Papa." She led him over to the car.

"Pa...pah," cried Luc as he ran enthusiastically to greet Diamanté. He peeked around the car door and stopped suddenly as if he didn't know the man who was seated in the front passenger seat. "Papa?" he said quietly.

"*C'est moi. Oui.* It's Papa," said the raspy voice.

Anna looked at her grandfather in horror. Diamanté was almost unrecognizable. His eyes were black and blue, his face swollen, and there were cuts and bruises all over his head.

I heard a noise and turned to see the dog, Max, come limping around the side of the house. His nose was lifted into the air. The old mutt had caught my scent under all the fishy-smelling clothing. I greeted him, and in one leap, he was on me, lavishing my chin with wet, slobbery affection.

Elise burst through the back door, crying. "*Oh là*, my Lobo!" She went immediately to her husband and threw her arms around him. "Are you all right?"

"Only a little *patraque*, *chérie*," he said patting her cheek.

"He looks more than a *little* under the weather," Anna said to me. I nodded in agreement.

Elise helped Diamanté out of the car and up the stairs. Anna and I followed with the children. She deposited the sleeping baby in the guest room, then came to stand beside me just inside the door of the master bedroom suite.

"He's looking better already," I whispered to her.

Luc ran over to his great-grandfather. He stopped abruptly at the side of the king-size bed, then held out his arms. Diamanté invited him to climb up and join him.

"You have a ouch-tee, Papa?" he said pointing to the bandaged leg.

Diamanté looked toward Anna for a translation.

"He calls all wounds 'ouch-tees,'" she explained.

Diamanté hugged the little boy. "It's not too bad," he said, "my 'ouch-tee.'"

"*Oui, mais*, just the same," I admonished him, "you will need to stay in bed for several days."

"Charlie, *mon Dieu*." Elise came over and flung her arms around me. "*Excuse-moi*. I was so focused on Lobo, I ignored you," she said tearfully. "All this time you've been gone from us."

"And missing everyone," I said, glancing at Anna.

Diamanté's face suddenly became grave. "You should leave as soon as possible. He'll come after me here, you know," he warned in a low voice, but Elise overheard the comment.

"Who will come after you, Lobo?" Elise said, alarmed. Her voice was loud enough so, next, Anna was looking concerned, too.

"I will tell you tomorrow, *chérie*. I'm too exhausted tonight," Diamanté said. Then he looked at all of us. "It's important to keep vigilant, however."

Anna seemed about to ask questions. I put my finger to my lips and mouthed, "I'll tell you later."

Her eyebrows rose. "Monique and Georges have a bastide near Grasse," she said. "It is large and very secluded. You could stay there."

"Monique doesn't like me much. Besides, that may be jeopardizing you and the children."

From the look on her face, I could see an inquisition coming.

"You'd both be safer elsewhere," Diamanté said. "Go, Charlie, get acquainted with Luc."

"*Oh là! Regardez le petit,*" Elise whispered.

Luc had fallen asleep in Diamanté's arms. As Anna bent over to pick him up, I stopped her.

"Let me," I said. She nodded. I lifted my son and gently cradled him in my arms. "He's handsome," I whispered.

She smiled.

Carrying Luc, I followed Anna into the guest room and laid him on the bed. The little boy rolled over and fell sound asleep. From the crib, we heard the soft, regular breathing of the sleeping baby.

Anna and I stood in the middle of the room. I put my arms around her and brushed her lips gently. Then I could not help myself. I covered her face and neck with kisses.

"You had better get a shower and a shave," she said quietly, pushing me away.

Her rebuff stung, yet I was reluctant to let her go. "Sorry," I said apologetically.

"We should leave first thing in the morning, as soon as the children awaken," she said in a low voice. "Get some sleep. We can catch up on the way." She gave me that direct look of hers. "I have a lot of questions for you."

"I seem to remember your saying that once or twice before. *Bonne nuit, amour,*" I whispered. "I'll be just next door."

"*Bonne nuit,*" she murmured.

After all the lights were out, and the house was quiet, I heard a gentle knock. I was so exhausted I did not get up to answer. I listened to the knob turn and opened my eyes. I wondered if I was dreaming as a vision in a white nightgown came over to the bed, lifted the sheet, and crawled in next to me. A familiar scent filled my nostrils, and my tired body awakened. I put my arms around Anna and gently drew her to me.

Chapter Twenty-Nine

Manos boarded the evening ferry for Nice. There was no reason for him to stay on Corsica. He had thoroughly searched the port and had come to two possible conclusions. Either Loupré had been killed leaping from the yacht or he had escaped Bastia altogether. In the latter case, he would be headed back to France.

As the ferry glided out of the harbor, past the burned-out, mostly sunken hull of *The Blue Amulet*, protruding like a giant shark fin out of the water, Manos thought about the first time he had boarded the magnificent yacht. It was while it was being built, and, despite the fact that his uncle owned it, to him, it felt like it was his. He had overseen its construction, named it, and painted the design on the prow himself, copying the amulet his father had hung at his neck as a baby to protect him from evil.

Manos had lived much of his life around ships, it seemed. His Anatolian Greek grandfather, Socrates, had been a shipping magnate, having previously earned a fortune in the tobacco industry in South America. Early in their marriage, his parents, Alexander and Anastasia, inherited a vast fortune and a fleet of oil tankers when Socrates died, unexpectedly, while sailing off the coast of Africa.

Nicolos, who was called Nicko from the time he was born, grew up in wealth. At the age of ten, however, he was touched by tragedy. On a Sunday in March 1977, both of his parents were killed when two airplanes collided in the fog on the runway of Los Rodeos Airport on the Spanish island of Tenerife. They had flown from the United States, where his father had concluded a business deal with the Port of Los Angeles, and to celebrate the success and their eleventh wedding anniversary, they were headed to the Canaries for a vacation. Their Pan Am flight was unexpectedly diverted to Tenerife when a terrorist bomb had exploded and forced the closing of the Gran Canaria Airport. While the diverted planes waited on the runway, a dense fog developed. Despite the greatly reduced visibility, the pilot of another Boeing 747 became impatient and attempted to take off. Neither aircraft saw the other, and the control tower, too, was enveloped in the fog. In the collision, the KLM flight ripped off the top of the Pan Am, and both aircraft were completely destroyed.

After the tragic death of his parents, Nicko was sent to live with his mother's brother in Calvi. André Narbon *fils* was a wealthy and powerful landowner who operated a large fleet of watercraft that he rented to the rich and famous who came to the Mediterranean to play. Nicko's uncle partied heavily and lived well. Unmarried, he had little interest in parenting, so Nicko was shipped off to a boarding school in France. Without his doting parents, and alone among strangers, the young Manos encased himself in a hard-shell cocoon. To the exterior world, he was fun loving and playful, but internally, he harbored sullen rage. His only visitor during those lonesome years was his grandfather, the senior André Narbon, a mysterious man whom, though he came very rarely, had the greatest influence on Nicko's life. A graduate of Saint-Cyr École Supérieure de Guerre, the elder Narbon had been trained in sabotage, guerrilla tactics, close combat, parachuting, and underwater warfare. He had fought in the Maquis during the Second World War, and worked undercover as an agent for both the British and French secret intelligence services. In time, Nicko had learned that his grandfather was also a terrorist, a man who could kill.

From the deck of the ferry, Manos stared into the black night sea. He had admired his grandfather, the only person whom he had ever trusted. The thought of him dying at the hands of a Loupré made him weep. Diamanté had said he didn't kill him, but he knew he was dead, so he had to know what happened and, more importantly, who was responsible.

Nicko had not been told about the blood vendetta between the Narbons and the Louprés until his grandfather's disappearance in August 1998. Extremely disturbed by the news that the Loupré family was suspected responsible, he vowed revenge.

Up to that point, he had mostly been a playboy, living on whatever yacht became available in his uncle's fleet, and partying the nights away, but, in 1999, following the footsteps of his missing grandfather, he joined the British Secret Intelligence Service as an entry-level special agent. In 2000, his training complete, he made *The Blue Amulet* the center of his operations, installing the complex communications and navigation equipment necessary. One of his first SIS assignments was to monitor the status of a man who had been given a new identity, a doctor who lived in the port of Bastia. Though he was never told why he was supposed to be keeping track of the man, he was delighted with the lightweight assignment. He could arrive weekly in the port, drop anchor, take the doctor to dinner, and invite him on the yacht to party. From time to time, he took on other assignments, too, as well as a load of contraband weapons whenever the opportunity arose. He drove a fast motorcycle, a Ducati, and women loved him. At the age of thirty-five, life was good, with the exception of one thing: he had not been able to find out exactly who was responsible for the mysterious disappearance of his beloved grandfather André. Until now.

***

As the ferry neared the coast of France, Manos left a phone message with a small private agency he had often worked for over the years. The company, French Riviera Security Services, whose badge had proven to be very useful to him, was located in Nice. The agency catered to the needs of the wealthy living in or visiting Southern France. He had occasionally provided bodyguard services for celebrities during the annual Cannes Film Festival and, over the years, had provided security guard protection for estates and yachts in Antibes. A local assignment would be ideal now. It would allow him to lie in wait for Loupré to surface. This time, he vowed, the bastard wouldn't outsmart him.

Manos leaned over the railing and looked down at the murky water. He knew he needed to call his uncle André next. It was the moment he had been dreading. Reluctantly, he punched in the number and waited for the onslaught of anger that would surely explode into his ear.

Uncle André's Corsican temper was well-known. Anything could set off an explosion. When Nicko received poor grades at the academy, the same Saint-Cyr École Supérieure de Guerre that his grandfather had attended, he was subjected to a full thirty minutes of booming lecture. He had held the phone at arm's length and still heard every expletive clearly. His grades improved, but if his uncle found even the slightest flippant comment offensive, he would explode in similar fashion. Nicko hardly ever telephoned him, and he even more rarely went to visit the man. He had planned, however, to deliver Diamanté Loupré to Calvi, alive, to prove to his uncle that he had finally done something to honor the Narbon name. Now, Diamanté was missing, having presumably been responsible for the sinking of *The Blue Amulet*, and there would be no doubt whatsoever who had screwed up. He knew his uncle would be furious with him.

"*Skata*," he said under his breath as he listened for the ring.

One ring. He inhaled a lungful of air.

Two rings.

Three rings. His heart pounded.

Four rings.

Voice recording. What luck!

Manos left a quick message to the effect that he was okay and that he wasn't responsible for the explosion and fire and, in fact, he didn't know what had caused it. There had been no recent mechanical problems that he knew of, and anyway, he wasn't even on the yacht at the time. He finished by saying that he was being reassigned and would be out of reach for the foreseeable future.

He hung up without committing to calling his uncle back. A wide smile spread across his face. At least he wouldn't have to deal with all the details of towing the hulk out of the harbor. His uncle's people would take care of everything. He regretted the loss of the motorcycle, but, of course, he already knew which model he would purchase next.

Chapter Thirty

Anna and I awakened before dawn, packed the sleepy children into the car, and drove quietly out of Castagniers. The village was deserted at this hour. Out of habit, I looked more than once behind us along the route to see if anyone was following. If Anna noticed my doing that, she didn't say anything. We did not talk much on the way for fear of waking the children.

We arrived at the bastide just as Monique was unloading boxes of fresh produce from the trunk of her car. She had obviously been to a farmer's market. The surprise in her face at seeing me was evident. Hadn't Anna forewarned her, I wondered?

She was very happy to see Anna, and the two friends embraced. Anna said something to her, and she lifted her chin in my direction, then raised an arched eyebrow. "*Eh bien,*" she said, a hint of disdain in her voice. "The missing man in Anna's life appears once again. When do you plan to make your next disappearance?"

I had not seen her for many years. *A pretty woman,* I thought to myself. *She would be much more attractive if she didn't have such a scowl on her face at the moment.*

"*Bonjour*, Monique," I said, raising my arms in mock surrender. I told her I was pleased to see her again.

She clicked her tongue, then politely accepted my proffered hand.

Anna undid Luc's seat belt, and he immediately awakened. His face perked up when he saw where we were. "Mama, can I go play with Rox and Rookie? Please, Mama?" he pleaded, climbing eagerly out of his car seat.

His mother nodded and watched him as he disappeared through the garden gate. "I'll just be a few minutes," she whispered to me as she scooped the baby into her arms. She gave me an encouraging nod and went inside.

Monique and I stared at each other.

"Do you want me to leave?" I asked after an uncomfortable silence.

She shook her head. "It is unnecessary. You are welcome to stay." A phone rang inside the bastide. "That will be Georges," she said. "Go around the side to the back terrace. I'll see to some refreshments."

She turned her back on me and hurried into the house. I stood alone in the driveway, wondering if I had made a major mistake.

***

It was late afternoon. The air was hot, and the sun was a brilliant yellow. Anna and I were together on the expansive back lawn of Beausoleil watching Luc as he ran free, making figure eights around the Italian cypress trees that surrounded the perimeter. The two dogs chased him, barking and wagging their tails.

Anna frowned and turned to me. She had freed her long brown tresses from the ponytail and changed into a black sundress that accentuated her suntanned shoulders.

"I've something to tell you, C-C," she said.

"Is Monique kicking me out?" I asked, fearing the worst.

"No," she said, laughing. She cleared her throat. "What I was going to tell you is something she mentioned to me earlier. Georges has hired a security guard for this place."

"Why?" I asked, sincerely confused.

"I told Monique what *Grand-père* said, about someone coming after you. I had to warn her, at least." She dug the heel of her shoe into the turf. "This is all so mysterious. I really don't know what to think anymore."

I looked beyond the garden hedge, toward the sunlit valley below. The Italian pines swayed in a sudden strong gust of wind.

Anna's piercing dark brown eyes were studying me. "I'd like to understand a few things, C-C," she said pointedly. "Is that too much to ask?"

"Look," I said. "I can't tell you all that happened in Corsica. That is up to your grandfather. You should know that he was taken in an act of revenge, and I helped him escape. We can't be certain if anyone knows I was involved, though. It is likely that they will come after him again. It has to do with a long-standing vendetta—"

She interrupted and finished my sentence. "With the Narbon family? I witnessed the whole event that night, you know. The night Elise shot his half brother. If she hadn't, *Grand-père* would have been dead."

This was new information to me.

"It was Elise who killed André Narbon?"

"Yes. It was a frightening night, creepy. I left France the next day."

"The concern Diamanté has is that you and the children could also be in danger."

She picked up a ball and tossed it to Luc, who ran gleefully after it, followed by the two eager dogs.

"So, it's probably for the best that Georges has hired that security guard after all?"

I nodded my head.

***

In Nice, Nicolos Manos stood outside the motorcycle dealer's showroom admiring his shiny new Ducati Monster 900. Stylish and fast, the Italian-made bike was engineered to handle itself around mountains. Manos couldn't wait to take it through the hairpin turns of Southern France. He was just about to put on his helmet when his mobile phone rang. Out of habit, he first checked the caller ID to make sure it wasn't his uncle. The caller was French Riviera Security Services.

"Manos here," he answered.

He was required to provide his badge number, then told to hold. He grimaced as he rapped his fingers impatiently against the motorcycle's seat. A minute later, a female voice asked in a businesslike tone if he had a piece of paper and pen. He breathed a sigh of relief as he heard the instructions. Lucky for him, she said, a request had just come in for a private security officer, a temporary assignment, just until the end of the month. The contact name, directions, and reporting date followed.

The call ended, Manos slowly closed the phone with a self-satisfied grin on his face. Grasse! What luck!

CHAPTER THIRTY-ONE

The following Saturday

Monique sat in a lounge chair on the back patio, the two dogs lazing at her feet. It was a peaceful afternoon. A warm Mediterranean breeze brought the scent of jasmine from the valley below. She listened briefly to the high-pitched hissing and whirring of the cicadas, then opened her book.

The tranquility was broken by the roar of a motorcycle coming up the long drive. Rox, the pup, rose quickly and dashed around the corner of the garage barking. Rookie, the elder, yawned, then got up slowly and produced a low growl as she lumbered after her errant offspring.

When the normally cheerful and friendly Brittany Bassets continued to cause a commotion, Monique closed her new novel reluctantly and went to investigate. Just inside the wrought-iron gate, under the shade of a stand of large plane trees, she discovered a long-legged, well-built man straddling a sleek black motorcycle. He flashed a wide smile at her, revved the engine loudly, then shut it down.

"Madame Durocher?" he asked as he dismounted and took off his leather gloves.

"*Oui*," Monique said, cautiously accepting his extended hand.

"Nicolas Manos. I've been assigned to guard your place." He produced a badge from the inside pocket of his black leather jacket, then looked up the driveway toward the former country house turned luxury vacation villa. "I do have the correct address, *non*?" His thick black eyebrows danced from side to side under his helmet as he squinted in the sunlight.

"*Oui, monsieur*. My husband arranged for your services."

"*Eh bien*," he said as he removed the helmet and hung it on the Ducati's handlebars. "Doesn't look like a place requiring heavy security, but he must have had his reasons." He flashed another wide smile at her. "Why don't you show me around, *madame*?"

Followed closely by the two suspicious dogs, Monique led Manos along the side of the house to the enclosed back garden.

"Beausoleil, as it is called, is a former bastide we renovated. It is quite large, as you can see." She pointed to the expansive back lawn, beyond which lay a small vineyard. "We have guests at the moment," she continued. "A friend is visiting with her two children. You will need to be extra vigilant with them. There is reason to believe they are in danger."

"Has there been a threat of some sort?" he asked, intrigued.

"I don't know exactly, but it's for their safety and, of course, mine," Monique replied as she led him back toward the front driveway, where the large three-car garage stood. "There is a small stone guesthouse behind the garage. You will be comfortable there."

"I take it you want twenty-four-hour coverage, then, *madame*? My instructions weren't clear about that."

"*Oui.*" She studied the amulet that hung just beneath his Adam's apple.

"If you don't mind, *madame*, I'd like to familiarize myself more with the premises. I'll try to stay out of your way."

Monique was a bit put out. This was supposed to be a day for herself. "*D'accord*," she said, abruptly dismissing him. "You may do as you please, get yourself settled, and so forth." Then she hurried into the house and quickly dialed Georges on her cell phone.

"He's here, *chéri*," she said.

"Who's here, *chérie?*" he said.

"The security guard. He doesn't look much like one, though."

"Why is that, *chérie?*"

"He just doesn't, that's all. I showed him around, told him he could stay in the guesthouse, and gave him the rest of the day to get settled in. The problem is I'm the only one here now. Anna and C-C and the children left this morning for Castagniers. They're to celebrate Elise and Diamanté's anniversary and will be staying there tonight. *Malheureusement*, I've given Pierre and Marie-Thérèse the weekend off."

"Will you be comfortable alone with the new guard, *chérie?*"

"*Non non. Pas du tout*, *chéri*. I just now locked the bedroom door." She went through the French doors onto the balcony. From her vantage point, she could see Manos in the distance inspecting the wall surrounding the property. "I don't know, *chéri*." She hesitated. "He's rather good-looking, young, well built, drives a motorcycle. He smiles all the time and tries to convince me he's charming, but there's just something disturbing about him."

"Well, keep everything locked up tonight, if that will make you feel better."

"He's looking around right now, and he's on his cell phone. Who do you suppose he could be talking to?"

"Don't get yourself worked into a panic, *chérie*. If it will make you feel better, I'll verify he's legitimate with the security agency, although they're pretty reliable. I've used them before."

"Oh, *chéri*, you're probably right. Maybe I'm just worried for nothing. *Je t'aime*," she repeated three times while blowing multiple kisses into the phone.

"*Je t'aime, chérie,*" Georges said quickly and hung up.

By this time, Manos had moved closer to the house. He was now standing curiously frozen in the middle of the kitchen garden just off the back patio. As Monique watched, he withdrew something very slowly from the inside pocket of his leather jacket and studied it for a minute in the bright sunlight. Monique gasped as she realized the shiny object was a small silver pistol. She held her breath as she saw him take aim. The loud *pop!* made her jump, and the dogs beside her on the balcony yelped.

The new security guard had shot and killed a small wild rabbit cowering in a row of purple basil.

Chapter Thirty-Two

This will be the perfect assignment, Manos concluded as he moved the Ducati to the side of the garage, then went around the back to find the guesthouse. He had checked the immediate grounds and much of the surrounding property. *C'est du gateau*, he thought, inwardly chuckling. It was going to be a piece of cake. All he had to do was put on a charming performance while at the same time acting the part of official guard on private property. What could be simpler?

His smile turned suddenly to a frown. One thing had him concerned. The woman who owned the property, Madame Durocher, didn't seem to trust him. He couldn't have her snooping around, watching him all the time like just now, wondering what he was up to. He'd have to make sure she was pleased with him. Maybe he'd have to come up with a way to convince her. As he thought more about it, a plan took shape in his mind.

He entered the small stone building Madame had called the guesthouse and surveyed the two sparsely furnished rooms. The bed was new and comfortable, but the place smelled musty. He opened a window and grimaced. Not the luxury suite with a sea view he was accustomed to on the yacht, but it would have to do. For now.

Chapter Thirty-Three

On Saturday evening, Anna and I joined Elise and Diamanté on the back piazza of the Ajaccio for a private late-night dinner to celebrate their fourth wedding anniversary. Lights twinkled along the hedges, and the table was candlelit and festive.

I looked over at Anna. Her eyes were sparkling, and she seemed to be enjoying herself. She was again in a midnight-hued dress. I wondered, briefly, if the choice of black was deliberate, a widow's resolve, or subliminal.

The waiter arrived with the aromatic *pièce de résistance*, truffle-dusted, spit-roasted lamb with rosemary potatoes, then wished us *bon appétit* and left.

Diamanté lifted his fork and knife. "By the way," he said, "there was a garbled message on the *resto* phone today. It sounded like Jacques."

"And it was, too." The familiar deep-throated voice took us all by surprise. We turned our heads as my father rounded the corner from the side path and stood before us.

"*Nom de Dieu.* Don't look so shocked, all of you," he boomed. "You should have realized I wouldn't miss this celebration."

Elise rose from her chair and proffered her cheek for a *bisou-bisou*. "Diamanté can't get up," she said. "He's been wounded in the leg."

My father shook Diamanté's hand. "So what did you get yourself into this time, you old *con*?"

"It's good to see you, too, *mon ami*," Diamanté said with a soft chuckle.

I was standing, waiting to embrace him. "I've been worried," I said. "Where have you been?"

He wrapped his arms around me. "I could ask the same of you, Charlie. The truth is, when you didn't come back, and they told me a *mec* was snooping around the hospital, asking about Diamanté and me, I got nervous and decided to get the hell out of there."

"Did you return to Saint-Florent, then?" Diamanté asked.

My father nodded his head. "*Eh bien, oui.* Just long enough to see to the *resto*." He looked at me, suppressed a show of emotion and embraced me again, then directed his gaze toward Elise. "Now, do you have any food to feed an old man? I'm starving."

"*Oh là! Mais oui.* Have a seat. I'll just be a minute." Elise hurried into the kitchen.

Anna had remained silent, watching the scene. My father pulled a chair up to the table and sat down next to her. Suddenly, he turned and took her hand.

"I'm sorry I acted as I did," he said, his usually gruff voice softened. "Luc is a handsome boy. I am proud to be his *grand-père*."

She nodded her head, but didn't speak. I saw tears along the rims of her eyes.

The waiter arrived with my father's plate and a jeroboam of Moët et Chandon.

As the champagne was being poured, I leaned toward Diamanté and said in a low voice, "The Durochers have hired a security guard."

Anna overheard me. "They fear we might be jeopardizing their safety," she added. "Do you think that's valid?"

Diamanté scratched the scar on his forehead. "You know what the Gypsies say about vengeance, don't you? 'Kill the one they love.' I have no doubt there will be an attempt to settle the score, sooner or later. When they find out I escaped, they'll come looking for me. It's only a matter of time."

My father looked from me to Diamanté, his eyebrows raised. He shook his head. "You shouldn't have returned to Corsica, *mon ami*."

"I vowed to never return, and I didn't for many years."

"I warned you over and over not to risk it," my father said. "The vendetta was sure to catch up to you at some point."

"Tell me. What exactly was the vendetta all about?" Anna asked.

"I first learned of it," Diamanté said, "when I was about nine or ten. One day, when I had received a particularly brutal beating from my stepfather, and to this day I can't recall having done anything wrong, I remember wailing that I wished my real father were alive. My mother broke down in tears, held me in her arms, and told me a story. It began in Castagglione, Corsica, a few months before I was born.

"On a clear spring day in 1924, her husband, my father, Jean-Pierre Dante Loupré, kissed her and Ferdinand *au revoir* and set out for the capital, Ajaccio, by way of the interior. It would mean a long walk through the thick undergrowth known as the *maquis*. The route was dangerous. There were wild boar, but that was the least of his worries. It was the bandits whom he feared the most.

"He told his pregnant wife that he would be back well before the baby arrived. She protested that she didn't want him to go, but they needed the money. He kissed her, and that was the last she saw of him. He never returned.

"The baby she carried was me. I learned later from my brother, Ferdinand, that our father had been killed on the way home, a victim not of bandits, as was supposed, but of the Narbons.

"Our mother was still young and very beautiful. Old Narbon, his name was Larenzu in actuality, had taken a fancy to her. I believe that's why he had my father killed. She didn't love Larenzu, but she knew she had no recourse. She was unable to support herself and two small children. She married him two months after my birth, and André was born nine months later."

"Didn't anyone suspect the Narbons had killed your father?" Anna asked.

"*Absolument!* The blood feud had gone on for years. It was a social code in Corsica. The term 'vendetta' originated there, and it was widely accepted. There had been violent attacks, houses set on fire, and other vicious acts of vengeance over the decades. My mother tried to keep us from knowing about it, but the boys at school talked. The vendetta between the Narbons and the Louprés must have been discussed a great deal among the families in the area.

"There were multiple attempts on my stepfather's life over the years. One, in particular, laid the bastard up for several months. I was too small to understand, but I remember a lot of shouting and *Maman* crying after undergoing more beatings."

Diamanté looked down, rubbed his gnarled hands briefly, then continued. "At the age of fifteen, I decided to follow Ferdinand and leave Castagglione for good. I took the ferry to Marseilles, where I lied about my age and got a job working at a metallurgical plant. The Nazis invaded France not long after.

"André, Ferdinand, and I were all members of the Maquis, the Résistance. André enjoyed killing, laughed as he blew the enemy's brains out. There was no remorse, no feeling, in him. Then there was another struggle. A grown-up one. Over a woman."

Elise was staring at Diamanté. He took her hand.

"Elise chose Ferdinand. They were married, and—"

Elise completed his sentence. "And then Ferdinand died in the war."

"Ferdinand was the strongest and the bravest of us all," Diamanté continued. "We were setting dynamite charges on railway tracks under a bridge. The German soldiers discovered us and opened fire. Ferdinand was the closest. He held them at bay with his rifle, motioning to us to escape. When all was clear, I found him lying in the mud, the back of his head blown away. André was standing over him. I had heard a lone shot after the German soldiers left. André had killed him."

Elise gave out a loud sob. "*Excusez-moi*," she said. I couldn't hear her words as she ran from the piazza.

Diamanté shook his head. "She had a difficult time accepting that story at first," he said. "She preferred to blame the Nazis for Ferdinand's death. But she knows it was the truth."

"Why did he kill Ferdinand? It seems confusing. What would have been his reason?" Anna asked.

"That's the part of the story I haven't gotten to yet," Diamanté continued. "It was to avenge his own father's death. It happened around the same time I left Corsica at the age of fifteen." He shifted uncomfortably in his chair and cleared his throat. "In Corsica, you see, the obligation to carry on the vendetta usually rests primarily on the male who is next of kin. Ferdinand was the eldest son. André made the assumption that it was he who had killed Larenzu."

"And did Ferdinand kill him?" Anna asked.

Her grandfather looked down. "*Eh bien, non*," he said, shaking his head.

"Then who?"

Diamanté didn't answer Anna's question. Instead, he seemed to retreat into himself. Sensing that he didn't want to tell us any more, I took Anna's hand and squeezed it.

Elise returned to her chair, and we all ate and drank in silence. For several minutes, the only sound we heard was frogs croaking.

Then the chef arrived to bid Elise and Diamanté *bonne nuit*. I looked at my watch and realized it was well after midnight. They had some discussion about the next day's menu, we all raved about the dinner, and he departed with a smile on his face.

Over small glasses of Farigoulette, the sweet thyme-flavored liqueur from Provence, Diamanté mentioned that when he was being held captive on the yacht, he learned, to his surprise, that the Narbon family still didn't know for certain what had happened to André.

"This is important," he said to us. His wolf like black eyes scanned the faces of those seated around table, and came to rest on Elise. "No one, absolutely no one, must learn who shot him."

I glanced at Anna. Her eyes locked on mine. After what she had told me she saw that night, we both realized that Diamanté had decided to protect the truth so that the Narbon family would not come after Elise.

Somewhat flustered, Anna took a sip of champagne, then asked me, "How did *you* get involved?"

I chuckled. "I merely helped him escape."

"But how did you know he was being held captive?"

"I didn't."

"So you just..."

I explained that after my father mentioned the vendetta, I searched the Internet and discovered, somewhat by chance, that *The Blue Amulet* was owned by none other than André Narbon's son. "I suspected that's where they were holding him, so I borrowed a dinghy and paddled out to it."

Anna, the raconteur, was looking for story details. "But, how did you know where..."

I lowered my eyes, hoping to dodge the question. "I'd been on that yacht once. It was pure luck I found him as quickly as I did."

For reasons of his own, Diamanté had warned me earlier not to discuss Nicko. He was very specific that not even Anna, Elise, or Jacques should know his name or about my prior friendship with him.

I went on to explain about our dramatic escape, Diamanté's being shot, and the experience on the Portuguese fishing boat. Finally, I smiled at Diamanté and said, "But, in the end, we got even."

He winked at me and put two fingers to his forehead in salute.

Elise's eyes grew wide. "The yacht!" she said with a gasp.

I made the sound of a huge explosion.

Anna put her hands to her mouth. "Oh my God." She looked from me to her grandfather. "It's no wonder you're so nervous about retaliation."

Part Four

Chapter Thirty-Four

Calvi, Corsica
Sunday

Fifty-seven-year-old André Narbon *fils* sat by the Olympic-sized pool of his estate overlooking Calvi on the northwest coast of Corsica. André's blue-and-yellow R44 Raven helicopter, his primary means of transportation these days, sat on the private helipad in the distance. Behind him, the thin, scroll-like Ionic columns of his elegant Greek-style palace gleamed white against the sea-blue sky.

He watched his new girlfriend, Chiara, swimming laps. The long-legged Italian beauty, whom he had met at a bar in Naples, had a figure that could match any of the marble statues of Greek goddesses that sat elegantly along the pool's edge. He decided she would do, for the moment.

He took a sip of his vodka martini and brooded. He had just returned from Bastia, where he had had to oversee arrangements for removing *The Blue Amulet*'s burned-out hull from the harbor.

He had lost ships before, only one other the size of *The Blue Amulet*, but that had happened at sea, so it was easier to dispose of. This was different. The mega-yacht was destroyed in close proximity to the port, near hundreds of other vessels, and, in addition, the police had informed him it was still considered a hazard since there were possibly more dangerous explosives on board. There would be an intense investigation, and the process could take months. What had his nephew been thinking, transporting munitions on a luxury yacht?

While in Bastia, André had visited Salim in the central hospital. The sole survivor of the disaster, his loyal chief electronics engineer lay fighting for his life, his dwarfish figure 85 percent covered in second- and third-degree burns. The captain and two other members of the crew had perished. Salim had informed him that Nicko had taken the yacht's only tender that night, leaving them to jump from the flames into the water. André had had to identify the bodies of the others. The memory of it made him sick.

Fat and pudgy from lack of exercise and too much booze, the bald, darkly suntanned, aging playboy took another gulp of his martini and ate an olive. It was the rest of the information that Salim had managed to tell him that troubled him most. Nicko had brought someone on board that night. Salim said he had recognized the old man in the beret from his early days in MI6 service. At first, he couldn't remember the name, his mind blurred by pain and the drugs they were giving him. Then, before he passed out, he had muttered, "*loup*," followed by an incoherent string of words about an intruder sneaking on board, gunshots, Nicko giving him hell, furious that the radar hadn't been on, Nicko grabbing night vision goggles and taking the tender…then an explosion.

André had received a short phone message from Nicko afterward, in which he claimed that he wasn't even on *The Blue Amulet*, which, he guessed, was technically true, but he was sure Nicko knew more than he was telling. And, now, he had disappeared, most likely to the mainland, and was not responding to calls on his cell phone.

André watched the lithe Chiara swim another lap. Her ruby- red bikini shone brightly in the sunlight as she skimmed just beneath the surface of the water. He stared at the bright blue Mediterranean just beyond the disappearing edge of the pool. If, as Salim had indicated, there were two other people on the yacht that night, where were they now? The only bodies recovered were those of his crew, and the only survivor brought to the hospital was Salim.

"*Loup.*" He repeated the word twice more. Then his eyes grew wild with anger. "*Putain de merde!*" he spat. "*Loupré.*"

He picked up his cell phone and hit the speed dial.

"We've a problem to take care of," he said in a low voice. "Pack your valise. The helicopter will pick you up in half an hour."

Chapter Thirty-Five

On Sunday morning, I wandered over to the Ajaccio for a *café crème* with my father. I wasn't surprised to hear that Elise and Diamanté had not yet descended, given our late celebration the night before. What did surprise me, though, was that my father had basically taken over the operation of the Ajaccio. He informed me that he had met early with the staff, telling them to be extra vigilant and report any suspicious activity or person to him immediately. It probably didn't seem all that unusual to them. After all, we were less than a month short of the first anniversary of the 9/11 terrorist attacks, and the entire world was on heightened alert. I was tempted to ask him whether they seemed concerned by his just showing up out of the blue, but thought better of it.

That afternoon, Anna decided to inaugurate La Cornue, and my father eagerly helped her raid the Ajaccio's pantry. I will never forget our little parade returning to the house, me carrying Isabelle, Anna pushing the stroller laden with groceries, and little tin soldier Luc marching along with a baguette propped against his shoulder.

While the children napped, and the air filled with the mouthwatering aroma of chicken, mushrooms, and tomatoes stewing in herbs, Anna and I sat in the shade on the back patio listening to the raspy hum of cicadas in the heat of the day.

She told me about her wedding to Mark, at my maternal grandfather's house in Obernai, about learning the recipe for the chicken cacciatore that was simmering on the stove from the housekeeper, Maria, and about *Grand-père's* death in 2000. Anna had become very close to Guy de Noailles since first visiting him in 1997. It was he who had helped her find her grandfather Diamanté and ultimately brought the two of us back together again.

I told her of my sadness the day I deserted her in California (yes, I apologized), and about my travels around the world in the months after that.

When Monique phoned to tell Anna that the security guard had shown up at Beausoleil, I suggested that it might be better if I not return with her and the children. She immediately agreed that I should remain in Castagniers, as she had just learned that her sister-in-law, Mark's sister, Adriana, was coming to visit for a few days, and she wasn't quite yet prepared to explain my existence to a member of the Zennelli family.

Later, after dinner, we sat together on the bench in the garden, white roses on the arbor over our heads glowing in the moonlight, and Max snoozing at our feet.

I finally asked her why she wore black all the time.

"It's all I thought to pack for the month," she said, looking genuinely surprised at the question. "Makes things simple. No need for decisions."

I decided to drop the subject.

As if on cue, just as we were having a glass of the region's sparkling rosé, we heard Strauss's *Blue Danube* waltz emanating from Clo's small house in the back corner of the garden. Years ago, our love affair began with a waltz.

"Seems like just yesterday we were in Paris," Anna said with a sigh. I took her in my arms, and we began to dance.

Her shining black eyes and her soft olive skin were irresistible. I kissed her. She didn't seem to mind. I leaned into her neck and smelled the musky scent of her perfume. Then I kissed her some more, pressing her to me.

A sudden flash of lightning in the distant sky, and the rumble of thunder followed by a soft susurration in the trees, shocked us out of our spell. Anna pulled away from me as droplets of rain began to fall, saying she had better go inside to check on the children. With the storm coming in quickly, Max and I followed her through the French doors into the house.

We had just reached the top of the stairs when there was an ear-bursting crack of thunder. We hurried into the guest room and closed the windows. The rain was soon coming in sheets, pounding against the windowpanes and frightening the children. Anna picked up the screaming baby, and I grabbed Luc's hand. We descended to the hall under the stairwell and joined the terrified dog, who had already taken refuge there.

We waited out the tempest and rocked the children back to sleep. Then, in the hallway outside their room, I put my arms around her and kissed her again. This time the kiss lasted a long time, and I felt her melting into me. My whole body ached for her.

I wondered briefly if she would have second thoughts. I didn't want to push her.

She unbuttoned my shirt, slid her hands around my waist and behind my back, then ran her fingers down the length of my spine.

I held my breath and whispered, "*Tu es sûre?*"

Chapter Thirty-Six

Anna didn't allow herself time to think. She just knew she needed him. As her fingers made their way down his spine to his buttocks, she felt herself coming to life again after the long year of agony and heartbreaking loneliness. She could feel his erection against her thighs, knew he wanted her. She wanted him, too.

"*Tu es sûre?*" he whispered as he suddenly pulled back and looked into her eyes, cupping her shoulders with his hands.

She nodded, and nestled her cheek against his. Yes, she was certain.

He picked her up, as he had done years ago, carried her into the next room, and laid her gently on the bed. Her clothes fell away, and she felt his mouth all over her body, then his tongue inside her. There was a sudden flash of light. Hoping there wasn't another storm coming, she closed her eyes tightly and momentarily listened for thunder. When she heard none, she drew in a deep breath, wrapped her legs around him, and pulled him in close.

They made love, holding on to each other, crazy again for each other, devouring each other, until they couldn't breathe, and, when they had finished, exhausted, still entangled and clammy, he turned his handsome face to her and said, "*Je t'aime*."

She ran her fingers through his graying hair, briefly wondering whether he would abandon her again, and if so, was she prepared to handle it this time?

Chapter Thirty-Seven

I watched with a heavy heart as Anna prepared the children for departure the next morning. She was wearing a casual cotton summer dress. Even though the color was of the same somber palette as always, the simple sleeveless shift was accented with a stunning slice of color—a bright burnt-orange asymmetrical hem. I whistled in a show of appreciation and told her she was ravissante. She laughed, telling me Monique had given the dress to her and insisted she bring it.

I bent down and embraced Luc, who, for the first time, didn't complain and even seemed to hug me back.

It was just after they drove away that Clo told me of the overnight intruder. From his cottage window, he had noticed the shadowy figure of a man enter the back garden from the garage side and quickly run across to the patio. He said it was just after the storm, and when he turned on the floodlights, the intruder had fled. I briefly wondered why I hadn't seen the lights go on, but quickly was reminded that Anna and I had been pretty wrapped up in each other.

I expressed my concerns that Diamanté and Elise might be in danger. He put up a finger, indicating I should wait, then went quickly into his cottage and returned with his shotgun, the one he used to scare away the occasional wild boar that wandered into the rose garden. The native Cambodian, who had lost his leg to a land mine in Southeast Asia, was accustomed to living in an alert state.

"I take care place," he assured me with a wide grin.

I went directly to the *resto* and informed my father about what Clo had seen. We agreed that I shouldn't remain in the house and that Diamanté and Elise should continue to stay at the Ajaccio, where he could keep a close guard over them.

I told him I planned to look into staying at the Cistercian convent for a few days.

As I turned and headed up the hill, the faithful Max followed me.

"*Au resto!*" I commanded him, pointing toward the Ajaccio. He gave me a soulful look with those big brown eyes. I bent down to pet him, then pointed again. He reluctantly obeyed, his tail between his legs.

Feeling entirely alone, I rang the bell at the huge entrance door of the convent. The portal opened slowly, and a diminutive woman, her face framed in a black veil, peered at me through tiny wire-rimmed glasses.

Soeur Sulpice opened the door just enough to let me enter and took my hand in welcome. It had been almost five years since I first met her, but the nun looked exactly as I remembered. A sexagenarian, she wore a black-and-white penguin-like garment with black sandals. A large, ornate filigree cross on a long silver chain completed her habit.

We had a brief discussion about my current situation as she led me down a long corridor with closed doors on either side. We came to the end, turned the corner, and entered a shorter hallway where she slowed and bowed her respect to a bronze statue of Saint Bernard in an arched niche in the wall.

Suddenly curious, I asked her if she had heard anything about the young woman I had cared for here, and the nurse and her husband, Florence and Geoffrey.

The nun turned to me. "Why, *monsieur*, didn't you know?" she said, her eyes wide. "They were all killed in a helicopter accident." She made the sign of the cross.

I was stunned.

She told me it was somewhere over the Mediterranean. There hadn't been much about it in the news, just that a military chopper had gone down with no survivors. She blessed herself again.

We reached the end of the corridor.

"This is one of the suites we reserve for visitors," she said to me as she opened the last door. "It is sparsely furnished, but comfortable. You are welcome to stay here as long as you wish."

I thanked her, entered the suite, closed the door, and immediately broke out in a cold sweat. Feeling dizzy, I went over to the washbasin and ran cold water over my trembling hands. The last time I was in this monastery was to visit a patient, and I just learned she had been killed, along with my nurse, Florence, and her husband, Geoffrey, the pilot of the helicopter. A long-forgotten detail suddenly came to me. André Narbon's body was on board the helicopter that day. When we landed in Nice, Geoffrey had whispered to me that their next stop would be "a remote destination to dispose of the cargo."

I stared at the bare walls and looked around the austere suite. The furnishings consisted of a sofa, chair, small table, bookshelf, and rug. I splashed my face with cold water. In the mirror hanging above the sink, I caught a glimpse of a man I didn't recognize: a haggard, graying man in his thirties with charcoal-gray eyes that were welling with tears. I went into the small bedroom and looked out the window toward Castagniers. The late morning sun was shining brightly through the Italian pines. I heard the monastery's bells ringing and checked my watch. Anna and the children were on their way to Beausoleil.

I couldn't stay there, even for a night. I opened the door and walked quickly toward the entry.

Soeur Sulpice was just coming around the corner.

"Is something wrong with the room, *monsieur?*" she asked, alarmed. "We can find you another, if you wish."

I assured her it was not the room. I bid her farewell and left the convent.

The disobedient Max was waiting for me outside the gate.

***

I went immediately to the house. The Mercedes I had purchased in Nice was still sitting in the driveway. As I retrieved the key from inside the garage door, Clo spotted me from the garden. I smiled and pointed to the car. He nodded, raised his arms to shoulder level, and pantomimed taking aim with a shotgun at an invisible target.

I saluted him, climbed into the car, and drove away.

En route, I called my father. I told him the convent wasn't going to work out, adding that I had decided to leave Castagniers. I didn't say where I was headed. He, in turn, didn't ask any questions, but reassured me that he would protect Diamanté and Elise. His last words admonished me to stay vigilant.

My second call was to Anna. I yearned to hear her voice.

"I miss you already, *amour*." I said longingly when she answered her cell phone.

She assured me she'd return to Castagniers after her sister-in-law's visit. I was tempted to tell her about the intruder at the house, but immediately had second thoughts. No need to worry her. We had a few days, and I assumed she and the children would be safe for the time being with the Durochers' newly installed security guard at Beausoleil.

A truck honked its horn in the lane next to mine.

"What was that?" she asked. "It sounds to me like you are on the *autoroute*."

I mumbled something about this being a bad connection and said I'd call her later. Then I hung up.

As I sped north on the A7 in the direction of Lyon, I put together a plan. My top priority would be to reestablish my true identity. Why haven't I done this before? I wondered. The inquiry had been conclusive. The decoy, I had just learned, was also dead. It was over. I could get on with my life. I called my bank in Switzerland and had them wire sufficient funds to an account in Paris under the name of Charles-Christian Gérard.

I had to be him again because I knew I couldn't live the rest of my life without Anna.

Chapter Thirty-Eight

Beausoleil

Anna closed her cell phone. She wondered briefly about C-C's call, but dismissed it as she drove into the driveway and parked her rental car next to the shiny black motorcycle.

Monique came running out to greet her. "*Coucou!*" she waved. "I'm so…so…so happy to see you, *chérie*," she said.

Anna unbuckled the baby from her car seat. "Does that belong to the new security guard?" she asked, nodding toward the Ducati.

"*Mais oui*," Monique said, making a face in the direction of the garage. "He's still sleeping, as far as I know. Some security guard, *hein?*"

Suddenly, a tall, curly-headed man dressed in black jeans, T-shirt, and high black leather boots appeared from behind the garage. He took off his dark glasses and smiled as he approached them.

"Well, *le voilà enfin*, here he is after all," Monique said, a tone of sarcasm in her voice. "Anna, *je te présente* the new security guard Georges hired to protect us."

He was definitely a handsome man, Anna thought, noting the square jaw, high cheekbones, bushy eyebrows, and sexy stubble of facial hair. She guessed him to be in his forties.

"*Enchanté, madame.* Nicolos Manos," he said, extending his hand and gazing seductively into her eyes.

"Pleased to meet you," she said cautiously. He was standing uncomfortably close to her. She quickly shook his hand, then stepped back. As she did so, something caught her attention: a talisman, hanging from a black leather cord at his neck. She stared at it. The amulet's design briefly reminded her of that on the yacht in Bastia harbor. She remembered what her grandfather had said about it being a common symbol in the Mediterranean area, with a lot of mystery surrounding it. What was this man's story, she wondered.

"Mama?" Luc called from the backseat, interrupting her thoughts.

Anna handed Isabelle over to Monique, then went around to the other side of the car. The little boy rubbed his eyes. "I want milky," he said as she lifted him from his seat.

With the baby on one hip, Monique took Luc's hand and led him into the bastide. "*Eh bien*, we'll have milky *tout de suite, mon petit*," she said.

The security guard lifted Anna's suitcase from the trunk of the car and followed Monique into the house.

When the others were out of earshot, Anna opened her cell phone and made a quick call. "We've arrived at Beausoleil," she said when Elise answered. "Tell *Grand-père* I've met the security guard."

"*Oh là!* Lobo says to tell you he wants to run a background check on him. Did you get his name?"

Anna raised her eyebrows. "He introduced himself just now, but I was so distracted by the children I've forgotten it. I'll find out from Monique and e-mail you." She hung up and walked into the bastide.

Inside, in the large country kitchen, Monique handed a cup of milk to Luc, then set a basket of fresh croissants in front of him.

Anna lifted the baby from Monique's arms. "The new guard is good-looking," she muttered.

Monique gave her a quizzical look.

"And a big flirt," Anna added, laughing. "What's his name again, anyway? I didn't quite catch it."

"Nicolos Manos. Greek, I suspect. Georges seems pretty confident about him," Monique clucked. She put her hands on her hips and added, "But then he hasn't met him yet."

Anna turned to her. "As a matter of fact," she said, "I didn't appreciate the way he sized me up just now. He did make me feel uncomfortable. I don't trust men like that."

Monique nodded in agreement.

At that moment, they heard the motorcycle start up and roar out of the driveway.

Anna looked surprised. "He's leaving?"

"He told me just now he was planning to go into Grasse for supplies. Said he'd be back in a couple of hours."

"When is Georges expected home?"

"I'm not sure. He was supposed to arrive today, but his younger brother, Serge, decided to drive down with him for a short visit, and that has delayed him for a day or two. You'll like Serge. He's quite good-looking, late twenties, a scriptwriter who wants to direct movies in Hollywood someday."

"Hum…" Anna said. "Adriana just might be very interested. She goes for the moviemaking types."

"*Possible*. Sooooo, anyway, *chérie*," Monique continued, her brown eyes wide with anticipation, "after the children go to bed tonight, you and I can have dinner on the patio, share a bottle of wine, and catch up. How long has it been since we've been able to do that?"

Anna laughed. "A long time, too long."

Chapter Thirty-Nine

In Grasse, Manos rode his motorcycle south on avenue Pierre Sémard searching for the perfect target: a transient who wasn't crazy or already drunk. As he drew near the Gare SNCF, he slowed down to survey the occupants of the street.

Spotting a homeless man next to a wall, he parked his Ducati, removed his helmet and gloves, and casually dismounted.

He approached the beggar with caution, looking for signs of the telltale bottle of cheap wine, the habitual drink of the French *clochard*, which would indicate the man had already been imbibing.

The vagrant was seated cross-legged on a filthy rag rug next to a black-and-gray shaggy-haired mutt, sleeping with its paws under its chin. A bowl of water, a white plastic tub filled with clothing, and a bedroll lay next to the dog. Placed strategically in front of them was a tin cup and a small handwritten sign, in black ink with all capital letters: SVP POUR MANGER MERCI. PLEASE TO EAT THANK YOU. He was no more than fifty, but his thin figure and leathery, sun-weathered skin made him appear much older.

The man lowered his bandanna-wrapped head and peered at Manos over the rim of his dark-tinted oval sunglasses. Suddenly becoming suspicious, he muttered something under his breath, then rose and quickly began to collect his belongings.

The dog stood, lowered its tail, and growled.

Manos halted and held up his hand, discreetly flashing a ten-euro note between his fingers.

"Want a job?" he asked in a low voice.

The man snatched the bill and stuffed it into his pants pocket. "What you want?" he asked uneasily, his voice coarse and gravelly. The fearful dog remained in place a few feet away, ears back and teeth bared.

Manos indicated for the man to follow him into a narrow side alley. The mutt gave a quick bark, then lumbered after them. The alleyway curved around behind a building and smelled strongly of urine and garbage. When they had reached a spot where they couldn't be seen, Manos reached into the inside pocket of his leather jacket.

The transient held up his hands. "Don't shoot!" His eyes were wide with fear. The dog barked.

Manos slowly pulled a folded piece of paper from his pocket and looked at the man with revulsion. He handed over the hand-drawn plan of the Durocher estate, explaining that he would pay him €400 to put on "a simple performance."

The man's eyes shifted uneasily as he studied the map. "Only four hundred euros?"

Manos's eyes flared. He grabbed the man's shabby lapel and, using his height to his advantage, stared down at him. "Okay, listen, five hundred euros, but no drinking. If you botch this, you won't get anything."

"Throw in a meal, and some food for the dog, and I'll do it."

Manos let go of the man's clothing. This vagrant was smarter than he thought.

"Now, repeat back to me what you are going to do so I know you understand."

The man dutifully repeated the scenario, and Manos, pleased with his choice, bought him and his dog a meal at a nearby café, then said he would see him shortly after midnight.

Manos's next step was to find a taxi driver who, for a price, would agree to take the transient to a point close enough to the bastide and wait for him. Manos had checked out the neighborhood on his way and had found just the spot he was looking for next to a tall hedge, under several large pines, just a few yards away from the wrought-iron gate that was always left open.

An hour later, Manos was maneuvering the narrow hairpin turns of the Gorges du Loup at top speed on his way back to Beausoleil. *In a few hours, if everything goes smoothly*, he thought to himself, *I will be Madame Durocher's hero!*

Chapter Forty

Later that evening, after the children had gone to sleep for the night, Anna descended to the first level. She found Monique and the two Brittany Bassets in the kitchen.

"Ah, there you are, *chérie*," Monique said. "I'm making us a *salade niçoise*. There's a crusty baguette to go with it, and lemon tarts for dessert."

They opened a bottle of chilled rosé and set the table on the outdoor terrace.

"Remember how we used to spend evenings together, laughing and gossiping, when we were students in Paris?" Anna mused nostalgically. "It was fun."

"Yes, it was, *chérie*." Monique sighed. "*Mon Dieu*. It seems like such a long time ago."

The full August moon rose over the garden, and stars shone brightly in the clear night sky. Anna wondered briefly where C-C was and what he was doing. Concluding that he was probably at the Ajaccio with his father, Elise, and her *grand-père*, she took another sip of wine and relaxed. She was happy for the first time in months, and looking forward to seeing her sister-in-law.

"What should we do while Adriana is here?" she asked Monique.

Monique was full of suggestions, and the two friends spent the next hour planning sightseeing excursions for Adriana's upcoming visit.

***

Manos stood watch from a dark corner behind the garage. He frowned and looked at the illuminated dial of his watch. It was already half past eleven. If the two women, and those pesky dogs, didn't go upstairs soon, his plan would be ruined.

***

The antique clock just inside the kitchen door chimed at midnight. Anna yawned. "I'd better get to bed. The little ones will be getting me up early."

"Let's leave the dishes. Pierre will be here in the morning." As Monique darkened the patio lights and turned the lock on the doors, she peered into the darkness. "I wonder where our security guard has been all evening. I haven't seen him at all. Have you?"

Anna shook her head and laughed. "Maybe he fell asleep listening to us."

The two friends wished each other *bonne nuit*, and Monique whistled softly for the dogs to follow them up the stairs.

***

By the corner of the garage, Manos breathed a sigh of relief.

Chapter Forty-One

Thirty minutes went by. The bastide was dark. When he was certain that everyone had gone to bed, Manos made his final check of the property. Pausing on the unlit back patio, he aimed his flashlight through the kitchen window and smiled. Monique's handbag was on her desk as usual. Everything was in place. He hoped the transient had not used the money to get drunk. He had given the taxi driver an extra amount to watch him, just in case, but who knew? He walked back to the guesthouse to wait.

Just before one o'clock in the morning, he was lying on his bed, half dozing, when he heard the sound of a window breaking on the back terrace. *Finally,* he thought with relief. He quickly rose and grabbed the wad of euros he had set out. Just as he was positioning himself at the designated rendezvous spot, he heard a loud crashing of dishes and a table falling over. Upstairs, dogs barked. A baby began to wail. Suddenly, his carefully chosen *clochard* came dashing around the corner of the garage. He flung the ill-gotten booty at Manos, snatched the money, and took off.

Manos began cursing and yelling after the man in French, Greek, and English. "*Salaud!* Κτήνος! Bastard! Σταματήστε! *Arrêtez-vous!* Stop!"

In order to make it seem like he was chasing after the thief, he stomped loudly in the driveway. After allowing sufficient time for the taxi to make its getaway, he edged along the hedge and into the road. He ran a short distance to build up a sweat, then turned around and walked back through the front gate.

***

Inside the ancient house with its thick walls, Monique and Anna hadn't heard the window in the kitchen being smashed, but both of them, as well as Luc and the baby, were awakened by the crashing sounds of dishes breaking on the back terrace and dogs barking. Frightened, Anna ran into the hallway and nearly collided with Monique.

"Stay upstairs with the children," Monique called behind her as she pulled on her robe and hurried down the stairway. The two dogs followed closely at her heels. "It's probably only rats. I knew I shouldn't have left those soiled dishes outside. Where is that guard, anyway?" she clucked in frustration.

Anna waited at the top of the stairs with Isabelle in her arms, and Luc hanging on to her robe. When she heard a loud scream come from the kitchen, she quickly put the baby back in her crib.

"You have to be a big brother to Isabelle," she told Luc. "Stay here with her."

"Okay, Mama," he said bravely.

She patted his head and kissed him. "I'll be right back."

Anna ran down the stairs. The French doors in the kitchen were open. One window had been smashed. Shattered pieces of glass lay all over the tile floor. Monique was grumbling something about her handbag missing and the security guard being absolutely useless. Anna ran to the front of the house and turned on the floodlights. She pulled back the drapes in the salon, peered out the window, and gasped as she saw Manos walking nonchalantly up the front driveway carrying Monique's handbag.

"Monique, come here," she yelled as she hurried to open the front door. "It looks like your security guard was on duty after all."

Monique came up behind her, and the two women stared as Manos climbed the front steps, out of breath.

"I caught up with the *mec* as he ran across the terrace," he exclaimed with a Cheshire cat grin. Then he bowed dramatically and handed Monique her bag. "I managed to wrestle this from him but, unfortunately, he got away." He feigned a look of concern. "Nothing missing, I hope?"

Monique checked the purse's contents. "Oh, *mille mercis*," she exclaimed. "It's all here."

"I don't think the *mec* will be back. I scared him pretty good," Manos said. He put his hands on his hips and cocked his head sideways. "Sorry about your dishes, though."

***

Perfect touch, Manos thought. *What a charmer I am.*

Anna's figure in her sheer dark blue silk negligee drew his attention. He glanced briefly at her mouth, then cleared his throat. "Mesdames, please feel free to go back to bed," he said. "I'll see to boarding up the window."

***

Monique thanked Manos again and closed the door. "I take back all those horrible things I thought about him," she muttered. "I can't understand it. We've never had a burglary at Beausoleil. It's always been so quiet and peaceful here."

Strange, Anna thought as she hurried back upstairs to comfort her children. *All of a sudden, a prowler shows up. And just shortly after a new security guard has been hired, too.* Was it purely coincidence? The writer in her made her suspicious. The handbag retrieved with everything in it. The intruder gets away.

Chapter Forty-Two

Paris

The drive to Paris took several hours. I kept myself awake with strong coffee along the *autoroute*, but I was exhausted as I pulled up and parked near the pont de l'Alma in the seventh arrondissement. It was just after three in the morning, too late to call Anna, and too early to find an open café. The Paris streets were dimly lit. The Seine was calm. Just behind me, the darkened iron latticework of the Eiffel Tower pointed majestically toward a cloudless night sky studded with stars. A drunken *clochard* walked past, staggering. He looked into the Mercedes, but didn't acknowledge me. Farther down the quay, I could just make out the silhouette of a pair of lovers sitting on a bench. I lowered the car windows slightly and pushed back the front seats so I could extend my legs. It had been five years since the accident in the eponymous road tunnel nearby. I thought to myself, *Diana's life wasn't the only one that changed forever on August 31, 1997.* I pulled my jacket over my face and fell asleep to the sound of water gently splashing against the bridge abutments.

Chapter Forty-Three

Castagniers

Diamanté sat in front of his PC in the upstairs salon of the Ajaccio. Along with his morning *café crème* and croissant with jam, it was his daily habit to check his e-mail. He brought up his inbox and saw that there was a new message from Anna. Intrigued, he read her account of the intrusion at Beausoleil the night before, and the fortunate ending, the retrieved handbag. She wrote that the newly hired security guard had behaved admirably and ended by saying that they were all okay, but, just the same, their nerves were a bit frazzled. Then this: *By the way, the guard's name is Nicolos Manos.*

Diamanté's eyes grew wide. *"Merde,"* he said aloud. *"Ce salaud de Manos.* That bastard." He stood and winced in pain as he put weight on his wounded leg.

"Elise! Jacques!" he yelled in a panic. *"Venez, tout de suite!"*

Elise flew up the stairs. "What is it, Lobo?" she called. Behind her, Jacques climbed the steps slowly.

Diamanté was leaning against the table. "Take a look at this e-mail from Anna," he said, pointing to the PC.

When Jacques and Elise had finished reading the message, they looked up, eyebrows raised and foreheads wrinkled in question.

"The security guard," Diamanté said, shaken, "he's a Narbon. The same *salopard* who kidnapped and beat me." He looked at Jacques. "We have to get Charlie. Anna and the children are in a great deal of danger."

Jacques scratched his head. "I don't know where Charlie is."

Elise and Diamanté stared at him as if he had lost his senses.

"*Oh là*. Of course you know where Charlie is, Jacques," Elise said, incredulous.

Jacques shook his head. "*Non*. He's gone. *Bon bref*. He called me yesterday. He's left Castagniers. I don't honestly know where he went."

"*Merde*," Diamanté spat.

Chapter Forty-Four

Nice, France

Adriana Zennelli arrived in Nice via the train from Toulouse, where she had made a stop to interview and hire the firm's new admin. The last of her business completed for this trip, she was looking forward to some time off. As she walked into the attractive central train station, the Gare de Nice-Ville, Adriana dialed the number of Beausoleil on her cell phone.

***

In the kitchen at the bastide, Pierre was cleaning up shards of glass, and, on the back terrace, Marie-Thérèse was doing the same with fragments of broken dishes. The boarded window gave testimony to the work of the intruder.

Monique, Anna, and Luc were seated at a table in the adjacent dining room having toast and jam. The ringing phone startled them.

Monique smiled and rose to answer it. "That will be Georges," she crooned as she picked up the receiver.

"Hi, um, this is Adriana Zennelli. Is Anna there?"

"Ah, *oui*, of course, Adriana," Monique said as she passed the phone to Anna.

"Hi, Addie. Are you still coming?"

"I've arrived in Nice. I'll be there as soon as I can rent a car. Just need directions."

"Have a pen handy?" Anna asked. "It's a bit complicated."

When Adriana said she was ready, Anna began, "Take the A8 as far as Cagnes-sur-Mer. Then follow the D2085 west until you see a sign for Le Rouret. That's the closest small village. Take the next right, and call us when you get to the double wrought-iron gate with a smiling sun in the center. It used to be open all the time, but we're under increased security since we had a break-in last night."

"Oh my God, Anna. You had a burglary?"

"The intruder smashed a back window and made off with Monique's handbag, but their security guard managed to retrieve it. The thief got away, and nothing else is missing."

"Wow. Lucky."

"Yes, I guess. Anyway, I'm glad you're coming. Luc can't wait to see you. How long can you stay?"

"I've got a week before I'm due to meet my parents in Paris. They're in Rome now."

Anna was quiet. She knew what was coming.

"Um, Anna? You know what I'm going to say next, don't you?"

"Do we have to go through that again, Addie?" she said finally. "I thought I made it clear to Zenn that I'm not ready."

"We'll talk about it when I get there. See you soon. *Ciao*."

Anna placed the receiver on the table in front of her. "Adriana's on her way," she said, a blank stare on her face.

Monique was watching her. "You seem upset, *chérie*."

Anna sighed. "Not with Adriana. It's my father-in-law. They're flying from Paris for the first anniversary of September Eleventh in New York City, and he's putting on pressure for me to go with them."

"You haven't gone to see it yet?"

Anna shook her head. For the past year, she had been unable to force herself to view the World Trade Center site where the towers once stood.

Chapter Forty-Five

Paris had awakened. It was a clear summer morning. The still air promised the day would be hot. I was seated at the Café de Flore, intrigued, as always, by the hustle and bustle on the boulevard Saint-Germain. My mobile phone rang just as the waiter set a *café crème* in front of me. I noted the number. Someone was calling from the Ajaccio.

"*Allô?*" I said hesitantly.

"Charlie." My father's voice was tense; something was wrong.

"What is it? Are you all right?"

"This is urgent," he said. "Anna and the children may be in danger."

"I thought they were safely at the bastide?"

"That's just it. Diamanté insisted I contact you. Anna sent him an e-mail. The name of the security guard? It's Nicolos Manos."

I caught my breath. "Did he tell you who he is?"

"*Absolument.*"

"I need to warn her *tout de suite*," I said, abruptly cutting him off. I speed-dialed Anna's cell phone number.

"C-C?" she answered.

"*Amour*." It was a great relief to hear her voice. "This is important. Are you someplace where our conversation won't be overheard?"

"No."

"Then call me back when you are."

I downed my coffee in one gulp, paid the waiter, and headed for my car. Just as I put the Mercedes in gear, my mobile rang.

"Okay," she said. "I'm in my room. The door is closed, and so are all the windows. Now, what's up?"

"I've had a call from my father just now. He told me you sent an e-mail to Diamanté? About the security guard?"

"Yes."

"And his name is Nicolos Manos?"

"Yes. What's all this about, anyway?"

"*Écoute*. That was the name of the man who kidnapped and beat your *grand-père*."

"Oh my God," she gasped.

"Try not to panic. For now, you and the children are probably safe. He's setting a trap, don't you see? Can you get out of there, on some pretext, as soon as possible? I am on my way."

"But where are you?"

"In Paris."

"Paris? But why?"

"I had my reasons."

There was silence. I wondered if she was pondering whether I had deserted her again.

"It's not what you are thinking, Anna," I said quickly. "I can explain. Just get out of the bastide immediately and call me when you are safely away."

I checked my watch as I drove in the direction of the Gare de Lyon in the twelfth arrondissement. I had just enough time to catch the 7:54 TGV to Nice. I thought to myself, *I am such an imbecile! Of course Manos would target Anna to get at Diamanté.* I concluded he must have known about her all along.

***

Anna ended the call. Her hands were trembling. She went into the bathroom and looked at her face in the mirror. She had to think quickly. She needed an excuse to leave Beausoleil. But what? A thought occurred to her. She splashed her face with cold water and combed her hair, then hurried into the bedroom and found Adriana's number in her cell phone directory. She hit send. The call went directly to Adriana's voice mail.

"We need to talk, Addie. Don't rent a car just yet. Call me back immediately." Anna scrambled to put together some clothes for herself and the children, stuffing them hastily into Isabelle's diaper bag. A suitcase would be suspicious. She tried Adriana's mobile again. Still no answer. She ran downstairs. Luc was sitting cross-legged in front of the television watching French cartoons and chewing on a slice of toasted baguette.

"Come on, sweetie," she said to him. "Time to get dressed. We're going to go pick up Aunt Addie. She's coming to visit."

Just as she lifted the reluctant toddler to his feet, her cell phone rang.

"Addie?" she answered anxiously.

"What's up, Anna? I listened to your message. You sounded stressed. I could hear it in your voice."

"Somewhat." Anna struggled to remain calm. "I had an idea. How about if Luc, Isabelle, and I come fetch you at the train station?"

"That's nice, but it's quite an imposition. I know I can find Beausoleil."

Anna cleared her throat. "Let me put it this way, Addie. We are coming to get you. Period."

"O-O-Okay. The tone of your voice. Is something going on?"

"Yes." Anna didn't say any more.

"You need to get out of there, and you can't talk, right?"

"Right."

"Ho boy."

"Exactly."

"So where do we meet?"

"I'll call you once we're on the road. Got to go."

"Okay. *Ciao*."

Anna hung up and went to find Monique, who was working at her desk in the kitchen.

"I've just been talking to Adriana," she said. "I think I'll take the children and go collect her at the *gare*. She's not used to these roads. I don't want her getting lost."

Monique peered over her reading glasses. Seeing Anna's pale face, she knitted her brow. "Are you all right, *chérie*? You don't look well."

Anna smiled. "I'm just tired and a bit hung-over from the wine."

"Should you be driving all the way to Nice in that case?"

Anna had a thought. "Would you like to come with us?" she asked.

Monique removed her glasses. "Well, Georges and Serge won't be arriving for a few hours. Why not? Just give me a minute to check my makeup and comb my hair."

"We'll meet you in the driveway in five minutes."

Manos was just coming around the corner of the garage when Anna drove the car up to the front entrance. He flashed his usual charming smile at her.

"Are you going somewhere, *madame?*" he asked.

Anna had a huge lump in her throat as she studied the man. What—who—had sent him here to Beausoleil? And why? Was C-C right? Could he be using her and the children to set a trap for her grandfather? What was his role in the strange vendetta?

"*Madame?*" he repeated. "Are you going somewhere?"

"We're just headed into Nice to pick up my sister-in-law at the train station. She's arriving today," she answered as calmly as she could, but she knew her voice was an octave higher than usual, and she felt weak-kneed.

"Would you like me to drive you?" he offered.

A shiver ran up her spine as she saw him peering at her two children in the backseat. *You SOB,* she thought. *I know what you're up to. If you hurt my children...*

She cleared her throat and forced herself to be polite. "No. Thank you. We will be just fine. Monique is accompanying us."

Just then, Monique came out of the house. "*Oui,*" she said cheerfully to him. "Pierre and Marie-Thérèse have left for a few hours to tour the perfumeries in Grasse. Why don't you take the rest of the day off also? After last night's excitement, you must be exhausted."

He smiled. "Well, that would be nice, *madame*. I just might do that."

Monique waved as they pulled out of the driveway. "After last night, I've changed my mind about him," she chirped. "We could have had a bad situation if he hadn't been here."

Anna frowned and pressed her foot on the gas pedal. "Monique, there's something I need to tell you about that… that…"—*creep, dirtbag, jerk, slime, sleaze, scuzzball*—"that bastard."

Chapter Forty-Six

I fidgeted nervously as I stood in line at the *guichet* of the Gare de Lyon in the twelfth arrondissement in Paris. The station was crowded. The smell of diesel fuel was strong. Out next to the platforms, I could see the *trains à grande vitesse* lined up for departure. I quickly purchased a ticket for the 7:54 TGV and checked my watch again for the tenth time. I would be in Nice in a little over three hours. My mobile rang. It was Anna.

"*Amour?*" I asked. "I've been worried."

"We've made it out of Beausoleil," she said quickly. "Monique's with us. She's terrified."

I assured her I would be there by midday, then hung up and immediately made another call.

"Anna and the children are safe," I told my father. "They're on their way to Nice under pretext of picking up her sister-in-law at the *gare*."

"Where is Manos? Is he still at Beausoleil, *alors?*"

"*Oui.* I assume so."

"If the *mec* is that dangerous, maybe we should call the *flics*."

"We don't have anything for them. Besides, I blew up that yacht, remember? They'd probably be more interested in me than Manos. Meet me in Nice in three hours." Then I added, "Inform Diamanté. He has connections we might need."

At just before eight o'clock, I boarded the train. I found a seat near a window and placed my medical bag at my feet. In no time at all, the cars began to move. I stared at the streets of Paris racing by and was filled with sudden dread. How was this vendetta between the Narbons and the Louprés going to end?

Chapter Forty-Seven

Adriana walked out of the Gare de Nice-Ville. The sun shone brightly in a cloudless azure sky, and the air smelled sweet with just a tinge of the sea. *The Côte d'Azur*, she thought. It was just as she had anticipated. She turned to have a look at the elegant stone façade of the seventeenth-century train station. It was an impressive sight with its sculptures and ornate clock. Feeling buoyed by the prospect of a much-needed vacation, she walked over to a kiosk and purchased a Michelin Green Guide to the French Riviera.

"*Bienvenu, mademoiselle,*" the vendor said, handing over her change. "Is this your first time here in Southern France?"

Adriana nodded and smiled. "*Oui.* I'm from California."

The man's face lit up "Are you looking for somewhere specific, *mademoiselle?*"

Adriana thumbed through the book's pages. "Just now, a café within walking distance."

"There is a shopping mall on avenue Jean Médecin." He took the guide from her and found the map of central Nice. "There, *mademoiselle.*" He tapped a spot on the page with his index finger. "The Nice Étoile." He smiled. "We call it Nice-toile. It's only a short stroll from here. Try Le Café Ritz."

"*Merci beaucoup*," she said. Pulling her suitcase behind her, she was off in search of the Ritz Café.

***

At the bastide, Manos went back to the stone guesthouse to change for his day off. Something worried him. Anna looked like she had wanted to get out of his sight as soon as she could. He had heard a distinct tone of animosity in her voice. What was bothering her?

Before he left, he decided, he'd have a look inside the big house. He'd been wanting to see the interior, but Madame had, so far, not invited him in for a tour. He quickly changed into a black T and jeans and put on his heavy boots. Dropping his helmet, leather jacket, and gloves onto the driveway, next to the Ducati, he went over to try the front door of the bastide. Of course, Madame had locked it. Maybe she had forgotten about the patio door. He went around the back. Locked also.

Undeterred, he carefully removed the boards from the smashed window and entered the large kitchen. It was clean and immaculate. He wandered through the rest of the ground floor, admiring the fine antique furnishings and exquisite eighteenth-century decor. Curious about the second floor, he ascended the staircase. From the hallway at the top, he spotted a baby crib through an open bedroom door. He wandered in and looked around. The armoire had been left open. There were a couple of women's skirts, a pair of pants, and a sweater, along with two pairs of women's shoes, but no children's clothing. *Strange,* he thought. He opened the drawers in a chest nearby. Empty. He scratched his head. Where were the children's clothes?

Next, he took inventory of the desk. There was a pen and writing paper, some postcards of Grasse, and an array of photos scattered on either side of an open laptop computer. Manos's eyes were drawn to a single photo, propped against the screen of the laptop. It showed two couples seated at a table, champagne glasses raised in toast. Manos recognized the men immediately. The woman, Anna, was seated next to Charlie Guilbert. The hated Diamanté Loupré sat opposite them, beside an older woman, whom Manos didn't recognize. His eyes grew wide. This Anna, Madame's summer visitor, was somehow connected with Charlie and that *salaud* Loupré.

Manos noted that the laptop had been left on, and, when he had bumped the desk, the screen saver had given away to display an open e-mail page. Addressed to Diamanté, it began: *Cher grand-père.*

The woman was Diamanté Loupré's granddaughter?

He read through the account of the burglary the night before and noted with interest his own name mentioned at the end. He frowned as he tried to put the puzzle together. If Diamanté was this woman's grandfather, why was Charlie in the photo? What was the relationship? It looked like a celebration of some sort. Charlie was somehow invited and, from the way he was staring at Anna, obviously captivated by her. Manos snorted. The man was always weaseling out when it came to women, and, all the while, he had a girlfriend. Suddenly it hit him. If Charlie was the granddaughter's lover, he had to have been the one who helped Diamanté escape from *The Blue Amulet*. Charlie knew the boat. He had a key to the stateroom! He knew how to get on and off without anyone detecting him. He even knew where the explosives were kept.

"*Skata,*" he swore in Greek under his breath. In a sudden fit of anger, he swiped the desk clean, sending the laptop crashing to the floor and the papers and photos floating down on top of it.

The phone in the kitchen was ringing as he ran down the stairs and out the front door. His mind raced as he hurriedly put on his jacket and helmet and started the Ducati. He was certain of it now. Charlie was the accomplice! He and Diamanté had been responsible for blowing up *The Blue Amulet*. This was the break he'd needed, his big opportunity to settle the score. What luck! Had he planned it, it couldn't be working out better. An evil, sinister smile spread across his face. *It's payback time*, he thought. He had to catch up with that car. The *garce*, "bitch," and those brats would be his bait. He gunned the Ducati and sped off.

Chapter Forty-Eight

At the Ritz Café on avenue Jean Médecin, Adriana ordered an espresso and a croissant, then picked up her mobile to phone her parents in Rome. Her mother answered.

"I'm in Nice," she told her, "in an incredible retail district near the train station. They call it Nicetoile. You've got to come here. Chic shops. I bought a Louis Vuitton bag."

Viola laughed. "*L'amor di Dio*. As if you needed another one!"

"I found a gorgeous pair of Christian Louboutins, too!"

"And how many of those red-soled wonders do you have now?"

"It's how I accessorize these drab business suits, Mom. Besides, I like shoes."

"Don't I know it! Anyway, how is Anna? Is she getting a good rest?"

"She and the children are picking me up shortly. I didn't have much time to talk to her earlier. She was in some sort of rush. How 'bout we call you tomorrow?"

"I'd like that. Kiss them all for me. Oh, your father wants to talk to you."

Adriana held her breath. Romano Zennelli had not been himself since the 9/11 attacks that had taken his son. The experience had been so personally traumatizing that he rarely spoke of anything else. And, of course, he cried uncontrollably every time he thought about it. On top of that, he seemed depressed, and complained that he couldn't sleep at night. The family had finally sought out professional help for him when he had taken a leave from his busy work schedule and, according to Viola, began spending his days isolated in his study in their Bel Air mansion. The parties and family get-togethers stopped. In desperation, his wife suggested a trip to Rome. Romano had always adored Italy. They planned to meet Adriana in Paris at the end of August.

"Addie," he said, getting right to the point, "I want you to tell Anna something for me."

Shaking her head, Adriana mouthed his next sentence with him.

"I want her to go with us to New York for the first anniversary."

"I know, Dad. I'm not sure she's ready yet."

She heard a moan. "We'll make it simple for her," he pushed. "She and the children can fly with us directly from Paris."

Adriana sighed. "*Bene*. I'll mention it to her again."

"Promise?"

Adriana promised, saying she had to get off the phone and call Anna to find out how much longer it would be. She ordered another espresso and dialed Anna's cell phone. No response. Maybe they hadn't left yet. She dialed Monique's number. No answer at the bastide either. An hour later, she still had not heard from Anna, and there was no reply to her voice message. She dialed the Durochers' number again.

A male voice answered. "Beausoleil. *Ici* Pierre."

Pierre? Who is Pierre? Adriana wondered. Did she have the wrong number?

She hesitated. "Monique Durocher, *s'il vous plaît?*"

"*Je regrette. Madame n'est pas là.*"

"Madame Zennelli?"

"*Ah! Madame* Zennelli *n'est pas là non plus,*" he answered.

Adriana's French was rudimentary. "Do you speak English?" she tried. "Is Madame Zennelli available?"

Adriana heard him holler. "*Oh là là.* Marie-Thérèse, *viens tout de suite!*" A garbled conversation followed, and then a woman's voice came on the phone.

"*Bonjour, madame.* Can I help you?"

Heaving a sigh of relief, Adriana explained who she was and asked whether the woman knew if Anna and the children had departed yet.

"My husband and I look after *le ménage,*" the woman explained. "We have been gone most of the day. No one is here at the moment, and Madame Durocher left no messages for us."

"Okay. *Merci.*" Adriana hung up. Another hour passed. Worried, she gathered her shopping bags and walked back to the *gare*. *They should have shown up by now*, she thought. What was keeping them? And why wasn't Anna answering her cell phone?

Chapter Forty-Nine

By the time the train pulled into Nice station, there was a huge lump in my throat. When I was in medical school in Paris, years ago, I learned that emotions can cause the structures in one's throat to swell. At the same time, tear ducts prepare to cry. I had not had this sensation before in my life, and, to be frank, I didn't believe it existed. To me, these feelings were both new and exhilarating as well as terrifying. I descended to the platform. The afternoon air was hot. I took out my mobile and dialed Anna's number. When I was not able to reach her after several attempts, I called my father.

"I've arrived," I said.

"We'll be there shortly."

"We?"

"Diamanté insisted on coming with me," he explained.

I hung up and called Anna's cell again, trying not to panic.

Chapter Fifty

Anna heard her cell phone ringing, but she couldn't reach it. Seated in the backseat between the children in their car seats, she felt helpless. Manos had chased and nearly run them off the road with his motorcycle. Scared they would crash, she had slowed to let him by, but he had pointed a gun at her, made her get out of the driver's seat, bound her hands with her own neck scarf, then pushed her, headfirst, into the rear seat. Now, he was driving. Her purse with the cell phone was on the floor in the front, next to Monique's feet. *Why*, she thought, *can't Monique hear it, or at least feel it vibrating?*

"Ah um," Anna cleared her throat loudly, trying to get Monique's attention. "Ah um," she repeated more forcefully.

Manos turned and glared at her. "*Taisez-vous!* Just shut up!" he yelled angrily.

Luc began imitating him in cadence. "*Taisez-vous!* Just shut up! *Taisez-vous!* Just shut up! *Taisez-vous!* Just shut up!"

Anna tried to quiet her son, but the devil had gotten the better of the three-year-old. He had a wicked smile on his face, and the more she attempted to silence him, the louder he hollered, which, of course, awakened the baby.

"Where are you taking us?" Anna shrieked.

"Shut up, beeetch!" Manos bellowed. His manic eyes glared at her in the rearview mirror.

Isabelle wailed.

"My baby is hungry," Anna yelled. "Stop the car this instant!" Seeing that the man was sufficiently distracted, she whispered in fast English to Monique, "My phone. In my purse."

Monique seemed confused.

"My mobile," Anna hissed, nodding and looking toward the bag on the floor by her friend's foot.

Monique's eyes lit up with understanding. "Oh!" she said.

The two women moved quickly. Monique found the cell phone and tossed it back. Anna opened it and hit dial. Then she handed it over to Luc, who, predictably, held it to his ear and proceeded to carry on a pretend conversation.

"It's merely a toy," she said, raising her feet to block Manos's flailing right arm as he groped behind him in an attempt to seize the phone from the little boy.

"*Ah merde,*" Manos said, infuriated. He slammed on the brakes, pulled over to the side of the road, and shifted the car into park.

Anna watched in horror as he flew out the door, leaving the engine still running. Before he could reach the right-rear passenger door, she leaned over and locked it.

At the same time, Monique climbed over the gearshift and quickly closed and locked the driver's side door.

"Mama, I'm scared," Luc cried out.

Outside the car window, Anna could see Manos reaching into his jacket pocket for his pistol.

"*Vite!* Get out of here," Anna yelled.

Monique slammed the car into gear, and they sped off.

Anna climbed into the front seat. Her hands shook as she tried frantically to free them from the scarf binding her wrists. In the rear window, she caught a glimpse of Manos, stranded at the side of the road, his pistol lowered to his side. A chill ran up her spine.

"*Au secours!* Help!" she screamed into the cell phone.

"Anna?" It was C-C's calm voice. The phone had, thankfully, redialed the last caller.

"Oh, thank God," she said. "Where are you? Manos chased us on his motorcycle and hijacked us. We managed to lock him out, and now we've escaped. We're on the D2085 just past Le Rouret. Oh, and C-C, he's got a gun."

Chapter Fifty-One

It being August, and the entire country seemingly *en vacances* in the south of France, there was heavy traffic on the D2085. Manos had run about half a kilometer, by his estimate, when the opportunity he was hoping for presented itself. He waved down an elderly couple in a dusty, battered old Citroën. They pulled to the side of the road and stopped next to a vine-covered, heavy stone wall.

"Can we help you, *monsieur?*" the man said, tipping his tattered straw hat. His was the face of an old French farmer, sun reddened and riven by time. The white-haired woman beside him wore wire-rimmed glasses with thick lenses that accentuated her blue eyes and chubby cheeks.

Manos flashed a broad smile at them. "I'm so sorry, *monsieur, 'dame,*" he said, bowing his head politely. "Could I possibly catch a ride with you? My motorcycle broke down."

"We can only take you as far as Cagnes-sur-Mer."

Manos smiled and nodded in agreement.

The trusting old-timer indicated to him to take the backseat.

Manos climbed in, but, before the man could put the car into gear, he pulled out his pistol.

"Get out of the car," he said, flashing a badge at them. "This is official business. I need your vehicle."

The woman started to protest.

"*Taisez-vous!*" Manos yelled at her.

"We'd better do as he says, *chérie*," her husband warned.

As the old people were getting out of their vehicle, a small commercial truck slowed and stopped behind them. The driver hung out the window and asked if anything was wrong.

Manos gave the old man a threatening look and warned him not to try anything. Reluctantly, the farmer raised his straw hat, smiled, and waved.

The driver nodded and went on his way.

"*Bon*," Manos said to the terrified pair. "My quarrel is not with you. You'll get your car back. Now, *vite*, give me your hat," he demanded of the old man. With that, he hurried to climb into the driver's seat and sped off.

Chapter Fifty-Two

I was driving my father's old Peugeot. There had been no sign of Anna's car since Cagnes-sur-Mer.

"We should have seen them by now," Diamanté said from the backseat. He'd been watching the road like a hawk for the past few minutes.

The traffic slowed, and we saw what was drawing everyone's attention. An elderly couple was staggering along the side of the road. I made a U-turn and pulled up behind them.

"What happened?" I asked. "Can we help you?"

"A man," screamed the woman. She had a thick German accent. "He pull a gun and steal our car."

I looked at my father.

"Was he tall, with curly black hair?" I asked her.

"*Exactement!*"

At that moment, the old man collapsed and fell to the ground. The woman put her hands to her cheeks and cried out, "Stéphane!"

At that point I had a dilemma. As a doctor, I was required by law to provide medical assistance. "Can you stay here and help them?" I asked my father. "I have to try to stop Manos before he catches up with Anna's car."

He nodded, then opened the door and got out.

"What kind of car was it?" I asked the women.

"A faded yellow Citroën," she replied, raising her shoulders. "A farmer's car, *enfin*."

I could recall only one vehicle of that description coming toward us. I had taken notice of it because it was going very fast and maneuvering in and out of traffic. It hadn't occurred to me that the man in the funny farmer hat behind the wheel could be Manos.

***

Monique was driving as fast as she could.

Both children were wailing.

"We have to stop," Anna said above the din. "Is there a small village nearby?"

"There's one not too far ahead. I can't remember its name. We were there once. It's a ways off the road, but quiet. We could at least gather our wits and calm the children."

They soon reached a byroad, and, without stopping, Monique sped to the right. Ahead of them, signs warned of roadwork. The pavement had been partially torn up, and the dirt roadbed was exposed. Monique was forced to slow as the turns became difficult and the car's tires kicked up dust and stones.

"Just ahead. That's it," Monique said finally as a small village came into view.

***

Because of the winding road, Manos had not seen the car make the turn. He sped past the byroad like a maniac wondering how much longer it would be before he caught up with the two women. Then suddenly, off to his right, in the rearview mirror, he saw a plume of dust. He turned the old Citroën around.

***

Monique parked near a small outdoor café in the center of the village. Anna got out quickly and hugged Luc as she pulled him from his car seat. He stopped crying.

Monique took the little boy's hand. "Come, *chéri*," she said. "Do you want to have an Orangina?"

He nodded.

Just then, Anna's cell phone rang. She was surprised to hear her grandfather's voice.

"*Grand-père?*"

"Where are you?"

Anna explained where they had turned off and stopped.

"*Écoute*," he said, "Manos attacked an elderly couple after you escaped. He took their car—a vintage Citroën, once was yellow in color. He may have followed you."

Anna closed her cell phone. "Take the children into the café," she said to Monique. "I have to hide the car."

She surveyed the village square. A fountain surrounded with flowers adorned the center. Just opposite sat a small stone church with a single steeple. A few people browsed the tables of an outdoor flea market near its entrance.

Monique took the baby and Luc into the café, and Anna moved the car to the rear of the church.

Seconds later, a vehicle matching the description Diamanté had given her raced into the square and screeched to a halt. The few people seated at the café's outdoor tables looked up at the noise that had disrupted their tranquility.

Anna ducked down in the driver's seat and quickly dialed C-C's cell phone number. Without waiting for an answer, she whispered, "He's here. He just drove into the square."

Knowing she would endanger the children if she ran for the café, she scooted across the front seat and got out on the passenger side. She heard the Citroën's door open. *Oh God,* she thought. *Now what do I do?*

From just inside the church, Anna watched Manos through the partially-open double wooden door. He stood for a few seconds in the center of the square, his hands on his hips, surveying the scene, then, apparently spotting her car, walked nonchalantly over to it.

Dialing C-C's phone again, she said softly, "I'm hiding in the church. He opened the hood of my car and threw something on the ground. Now he's just standing there looking around. The children and Monique are inside the café. Oh no! He's walking in the direction of the café!"

She didn't hear a response. She looked at her cell phone. The battery was dead. Damn. She had forgotten to charge it that morning. She threw it down and ran frantically to the back of the church. A priest was just coming into the sanctuary.

"I need your help, Father," she pleaded.

Chapter Fifty-Three

From the rear table in the café where she was seated, Monique caught a glimpse of Manos coming across the square.

"*Viens, petit.* Come," she said, quickly getting up and grabbing Luc's hand. With the baby under one arm, she pulled the reluctant toddler toward the kitchen.

A chef was arranging a platter of *crudités* at the counter. "*Madame,*" he said, "I'm sorry, but you can't be in here."

"I need to exit the back door, immediately," she explained. "Please understand. This is very urgent. A man has just entered the café…" She took in a breath. "He is threatening us."

Seeing the look of panic in Monique's eyes, the chef quickly opened the rear door for her. Grabbing a cleaver from his collection of knives, he said, "I'll take care of this. Don't worry, *madame.*" He closed the door quietly and hurried into the bar. Behind the zinc bar, a tall man was speaking with the bartender.

When the stranger started toward the kitchen, the chef blocked the way with his stout frame. Pointing with the cleaver toward the opposite corner of the bar where the restrooms were located, he said, "*Les toilettes sont par là, monsieur.*"

"Sorry to bother you, *monsieur*," Manos said, quickly flashing his security guard badge at the man. "Have you seen a woman with a baby and a small child this afternoon? I am looking for them."

The chef studied Manos's face. "We have seen no one," he said finally.

Manos nodded in the bartender's direction. "But he said—"

"He was mistaken, *monsieur*."

Manos's black eyes scrutinized the man. "My wife," he said with a slightly pathetic sob, "has kidnapped my children. Please help me. She is not rational. I need to get them away from her before she hurts them."

"I...I didn't..." the chef stammered. "I didn't realize it was a family affair." He pointed toward the kitchen and said, "*Par là*. They went through the rear door."

***

Pulling the protesting Luc behind her, Monique hurried as quickly as she could away from the café.

A priest approached them. "*Madame*," he said, "your friend is in the church. Come with me." He picked up Luc and ran, with Monique and the baby following close behind. Once inside the sanctuary, he set Luc down and closed the heavy wooden door.

"Mama!" Luc yelled, running into his mother's arms.

"Manos came into the café," Monique whispered to Anna. "It's only a matter of time before he figures out where we are."

***

With fear in my heart, I stopped the car at the periphery of the square. It was a small village. The Citroën was parked in the center. I did not see Manos or Anna and the children anywhere.

Diamanté surveyed the tranquil scene with his wolf like eyes. "He could be in that café," he said finally.

"Stay here," I said. "Your wounded leg will hold us back. Besides, it's better he not see you." I tossed him my mobile. "Call the *flics*. I'll go have a look inside."

He nodded, then opened the rear passenger window and, crouching low in the back seat, placed the World War II–era Walther PP he had brought with him in shooting position.

"*Bon courage*," he said. "The man is dangerous."

As I got out of the car, I tried to calm my nerves. Could I really assume Nicko didn't know about my involvement in the destruction of *The Blue Amulet*?

Chapter Fifty-Four

Adriana Zennelli was by now really worried. Where were Anna and the children? They should have arrived in Nice two hours ago. She couldn't reach Anna's cell phone, and no one at Beausoleil seemed to have heard from Anna or Monique. She returned to the train station and rented a car. She wasn't entirely clear what she would do next, but she felt she had to do something.

She took out the notes she had made when Anna had given her directions, set them in front of her on the dash, and started the car.

"Okay, Anna, girl, I'm coming to find you and the little ones," she said aloud as she put the car in gear, thinking of her brother, Mark. "Dear God, I hope they're all okay."

Chapter Fifty-Five

In the sacristy, Monique shifted baby Isabelle to her shoulder and fumbled for her cell phone in her shoulder bag. Not finding it, she grabbed the church's phone and dialed Georges's cell. He answered on the third ring.

"*Chéri*," she said frantically. "*C'est moi. Nous sommes piégés.*"

"Trapped? But how? What?"

"*Écoute.* The security guard...tried to kidnap us. Oh, *chéri*, I am so scared."

Georges pulled the Mercedes over. "Neecque, Neecque," he repeated. It was the nickname he used for her when he wanted her to calm down. "Tell me, Neecque, what's going on? Where are you, exactly?"

"Remember that little village? Where we stopped for a *café crème* and thought the square was charming?"

"The Sunday we decided to purchase Beausoleil?"

"*Oui, oui, oui!* That's it. We're hiding in the church."

"I think I can find it again. We're coming the scenic route, unfortunately, and there's a lot of traffic. Serge wanted to do the August tourist thing."

***

Georges looked at his younger brother, who had seized the opportunity to step out of the car and have a smoke.

"Serge," he hollered as he put the Mercedes in gear. "Get in the car! *Vite!*"

"What the..." Serge ground the cigarette into the dirt with his heel and hopped back in the seat. He was still closing the door when Georges took off at high speed.

"Okay, Neeque," Georges was saying, "stay on the phone. Tell me what's happening."

The phone went dead. He looked at the number and redialed. There was only a busy signal.

"*Merde*," he said.

Serge had been watching his brother. "What's going on? Is Monique in some sort of trouble?"

Georges nodded. "I think we'd better get to her as soon as possible." He swore again. "Damned traffic. I knew we shouldn't have come this way."

Serge raked his hands through his hair. "Sorry," he said.

"It wouldn't have made a difference, ordinarily," Georges mumbled as he tried Monique's cell phone. It went immediately to voice mail. "*Merde*. Her cell's off." He handed the phone to Serge. "Keep redialing this number."

Chapter Fifty-Six

The café was called Chez Vincent. Its façade was painted bright golden yellow, and a large ochre-colored awning shielded the terrace from the midafternoon sun. As I approached the entrance, my mind concentrating on how to diffuse the situation with Nicko, I passed a young couple seated at a table having a cool drink. Just outside the door, a black chalkboard on an easel advised patrons of the *Plat du Jour*. Scrawled in bright lime green were the letters *Poulet rôti*. The smell of chicken roasting filled my nostrils as I entered.

I looked around for Anna and the children, but they were not there. Neither was Nicko. In fact, I was surprised that there were no patrons at all. The restaurant was deserted. Multicolored blue, yellow, and red table linens adorned small wooden tables. Antique lamps hung from the ceiling. There was an enormous reproduction of Vincent Van Gogh's *Café Terrace at Night* painted on the wall. Hearing voices, I walked around to the bar at the back.

The bartender was standing behind the zinc, nervously wringing his hands. With him was the portly chef, who was speaking loudly into the phone. I heard him yell, "*Oui! Oui! Oui! Venez tout de suite!* Come immediately!" Then he slammed down the receiver.

"Have you, by any chance, seen a woman with two children?" I asked them.

"Ah, *oui*, in actuality," the bartender replied, blowing air through his lips in disgust. "She left. Next her husband arrived." He tossed his arms in the air and sniffed. "He snatched a knife from Armand."

"Her husband?" I scratched my head.

"He was very upset," he said, pointing toward the rear of the café. "Followed her out the kitchen door."

Chapter Fifty-Seven

They were startled by the sound of loud footsteps in the hall. Then, suddenly, the sacristy door opened with hurricane force, and the shadowy figure of Manos stood, framed in the doorway, wielding a gun in one hand and a heavy kitchen cleaver in the other.

"*Enfin*. I've found what I've been looking for!" he said.

Monique screamed.

"*Monsieur!*" yelled the terrified priest. "You must leave this church at once!"

With his elbow, Manos shoved the diminutive man aside, causing him to crash violently against an armoire.

The situation was desperate. Anna knew she had to do something. Even though Manos was much taller, she grabbed for the hand holding the cleaver. If only she could dislodge and cause him to drop it. She hit the back of his arm hard, but he was too strong for her. He swung the blade around, grazing the flesh of her arm just above the elbow. Blood spurting from the wound, she grabbed at the cleaver again. This time, she held on with all her strength while, at the same time, kicking Manos's legs. Manos tried to maneuver the butt of the gun to hit her over her head, but he had all he could do to fend off the woman.

As she watched the struggle in horror, Monique, still holding baby Isabelle, quickly grabbed Luc's hand and edged slowly toward the open door. With Manos preoccupied, she maybe had a chance to get the children away.

Just as the three made it out of the church, Luc broke loose and ran back in, yelling, "Mama!" at the top of his voice.

With the baby in her arms, Monique ran frantically to the rental car. She put Isabelle into her car seat and quickly climbed behind the steering wheel. The vehicle wouldn't start. Wild-eyed and desperate, she saw an old man, with one leg in a cast, limping toward them. He waved his arms and called out, but she couldn't quite understand what he was saying. Just then, she spotted her missing cell phone on the floor of the front seat. She grabbed it and quickly speed-dialed Georges's number.

Serge answered. "Monique! *Salut, chérie. Ça va?*"

"Give the phone to Georges!" she hissed.

There was a short conversation, and Georges came on.

"What's happened?" he said.

"I got the baby out. I'm in the car, but it won't start."

"We're just about there. Can you get someone to help you?"

Just then Diamanté reached the car. "Monique? I'm Anna's grandfather," he said quickly, pointing to the Peugeot. "Take our car. Get the baby out of here."

"Monique?" Georges was saying into the phone.

"Anna's grandfather is here. He's trying to help," she said. "I'll call you back."

Monique hefted the baby, in her car carrier, into the rear seat of the Peugeot and climbed in. Diamanté grabbed his Walther and closed the car door.

"Anna and Luc are still in the church," Monique said as she started the engine. With that, she gunned the car and sped away from hell.

***

In the sacristy, Anna let go of the cleaver and turned her back to Manos in a futile attempt to shield her son. Manos hurled the heavy steel knife through a small glass window, shattering it. Then he grabbed Anna and tossed her against a large wooden desk. She lay limp, Luc crying and holding on to her. Manos then scooped up the boy and ran.

***

Diamanté spun around. He didn't care whether his leg hurt or not. He had to save Anna and Luc. And where was Charlic? His wolf like eyes surveyed the square. The marketplace was now deserted. He moved as quickly as he could to the front door of the church. Finding it locked, he edged his way along the façade and peered around the corner of the building. That's when he saw Manos running from the church's side door, carrying Luc.

With his Walther raised, Diamanté stepped forward into his path.

Manos stopped.

"*Eh bien*, if it isn't *l'enculé* himself," Manos said. A wide Cheshire cat grin spread over his face. "I've been waiting for you, *salaud*."

"Papa!" Luc yelled.

"Stay calm, *petit*," Diamanté said softly. "You'll be okay." Then he said to Manos, "Let the boy go. It's me you want."

"Oh, but don't be so sure, *viellard*," Manos replied, deliberately prolonging eye contact with the old man. "He's your flesh and blood, isn't he? I guessed it. The woman is your granddaughter, *non*? Now, I settle the vendetta." He held the pistol against the little head.

"*Non!*" Diamanté yelled. "You will not do this!"

Manos turned the pistol toward Diamanté and immediately pulled the trigger.

The Walther dropped from the old man's hand as he slumped to the ground.

Chapter Fifty-Eight

Full of apprehension, I made my way past countertops strewn with vegetables, and racks filled with pots and pans. The rear door had been left open, and, just as I stepped outside, I heard Diamanté yelling, "You will not do this!"

Then, the sound of a shot.

In a panic, I rushed toward the church. Diamanté was sprawled on the ground. I caught a glimpse of Manos running with Luc in his arms toward the yellow Citroën in the center of the square. The Peugeot was gone. *Where was Anna?* I wondered. I picked up Diamanté's gun, but it was futile. The car's tires screeched, and it was already out of range.

I kneeled over Diamanté and felt a faint pulse. There was blood oozing from under his shirt. I quickly pulled up his clothing and examined his right upper torso. This time, I thought to myself, Manos meant to kill him.

Diamanté's eyes fluttered open slightly, and he tried to talk. "Anna...in church," he gasped between short breaths. "Manos...Luc. Monique escape...with baby."

A few curious villagers gathered around us. We heard sirens in the distance.

"Hold on, *mon ami*," I whispered to him. "Medics are on the way."

"Phone," he said in a raspy, low voice.

I didn't understand. "Phone…urgent…" He was passing in and out of consciousness.

I guessed that he was talking about my mobile phone. I fished it from his shirt pocket.

"Go…" He pushed me away. "Help Anna."

As I entered the church, a priest pointed me to the sacristy, where I found Anna slumped on the floor. Her arm was bleeding, and she was moaning and holding her head. I removed my belt and immediately applied a tourniquet.

"C-C?" Her eyes were unable to focus. She tried to get up. "Where is Luc? And the baby? Where is Isabelle?" she mumbled.

I helped her to stand. We made it to the door of the church just as the police cars and SAMU, sirens bleating, came screaming into the square.

Without delay, Diamanté was put on a stretcher and into the back of the ambulance.

"The bullet is probably lodged in his right lung," I told the doctor tending to him. They would be taking him immediately to Grasse Hospital for surgery, he informed me.

Anna, too, would need swift attention for her arm. I helped her climb into the front seat. Again, she mumbled something about the children. I did not know what to tell her.

"Your *grand-père* said Monique has them," I said finally. "She must have taken the Peugeot."

She seemed satisfied with that answer. I closed the door and watched the SAMU depart. I was immediately hit by an attack of guilt. *Had I done the right thing,* I wondered, *in not telling her about Luc?*

I focused on the activities around me. The *flics* were everywhere. One of them was interviewing the restaurateur. Two were doing a thorough search of Anna's car. I went over to them as they pulled out a bag of children's clothing. Did I know what happened, they asked me. I identified myself and did my best to fill them in quickly, especially the part about Luc being kidnapped. I described the Citroën and told them it was urgent that we find the boy. They went into immediate action on this information. They called in the description of the car, and one of them jumped into his vehicle and took off, lights flashing and siren blaring.

A sleek black roadster entered the square and skidded to a stop. I recognized it as a Mercedes SL55 AMG. It was Georges's. He and another man stepped quickly out of the car. Monique had called him, he said. I was relieved to hear that she was on her way back to Beausoleil with Isabelle. He introduced his brother, Serge. He looked like Georges, but he was younger.

"We are losing time," I told them. "Did you meet an old farmer's car, a Citroën, when you drove in just now?"

Georges gave his brother a look. They told me they had remarked about that vehicle, actually, because it was going uncharacteristically fast.

"Did you see which way it went?"

Serge recalled the car turned left onto the main road.

"I need your help," I told them. "Luc has been kidnapped."

"*Mon Dieu*," they gasped in unison.

We heard the *wop wop* sound of a helicopter flying low over the village.

Georges, Serge, and I climbed into the roadster and sped off.

Chapter Fifty-Nine

Grasse Hospital

Her arm in a sling, Anna sat on a bed in the emergency ward holding an ice pack to her forehead. The distinctive hospital smell of rubbing alcohol combined with human excretions made her feel sick to her stomach.

"How is my grandfather?" she asked the nurse in a shaky voice.

"Still in surgery, *madame*."

"I...I need to call his wife. Is there a phone I can use?"

The woman helped her into a wheelchair and pushed her to the emergency room's front desk. Anna lifted the receiver and dialed the Ajaccio.

"Elise, *s'il vous plaît*," she said quickly when the sous-chef answered. "*C'est urgent*."

Anna heard the clamor and commotion of the restaurant's kitchen in the background, and then Elise came on. "*Oh là*. Anna? I've been so worried. Where are you? Where is Lobo?"

"*Grand-père* and I are at Grasse Hospital. He's in surgery."

The woman screamed into the phone. "What happened?"

"He has been shot. I'm told he'll be okay."

"I'm coming immediately!" Elise said, adding, "Oh, *mon Dieu*, Anna. Where is Jacques?"

"I...I don't know." Anna tried to think. The painkiller she had been given was starting to take effect. "I haven't seen him."

"*Mais*, that's strange. They left here together to pick up Charlie at the *gare*. Oh, *mon Dieu!*"

"Just come right away, Elise. *Grand-père* needs you."

The mention of the train station reminded Anna that she'd entirely forgotten about her sister-in-law. She dialed Adriana's cell phone.

"Addie? It's Anna."

"Oh my God, I've been so worried about you."

"I'm so sorry, Addie. Are you still in Nice?"

"No, I finally gave up and rented a car. I'm on my way. Why didn't you call me?"

"My cell phone went dead. Addie, listen. Can you pick me up? I'm in Grasse. It's only about another ten kilometers. Now, don't panic at what I'm about to say. I'm at the hospital."

She heard Adriana gasp.

"I don't have time to explain. It won't be hard to find. Just follow the signs."

Adriana said she'd be there as soon as she could. Anna's hands shook as she hung up and quickly dialed the bastide.

"Has Monique arrived?" she asked when Pierre answered.

"*Oui, madame.*"

"Anna, *chérie*." Monique's voice was shrill. "Are you all right? Where are you?"

"At the hospital. I've a badly cut arm and a mild concussion. It was awful. I'm so glad you were able to escape with the children."

"Children? Anna, I only have Isabelle here with me. Don't you remember? Luc ran back to you."

Anna's mind whirled. "What?" she shrieked.

"He ran into the church. I thought you had him."

It came back to Anna like a flash of lightning. In an instant, she saw it all: the horror of trying to shield her son, being thrown to the floor, hitting her head.

"I don't remember what happened after…Oh my God, Monique, I don't know where Luc is!"

"Your grandfather was there. Maybe he knows."

"He's in surgery. He was shot."

"*Mon Dieu!*"

Anna felt a panic attack coming on. "The police were there when we left. Maybe they've already found Luc. I need to let C-C know at once." She hesitated. "I…I can't seem to remember the number of his mobile. Can you go upstairs to my room? It's on a piece of paper somewhere on the desk."

"*Attends.*"

Anna could hear the *thump thump* of Monique's feet as she ran up the stairs.

"*Mon Dieu*, Anna. Someone has been in this room. Everything is turned upside down."

Anna tried to make sense of what Monique was saying. "Do you think it was Manos? What could he have been looking for?"

"I don't know, *chérie*. Pierre said the boards had been removed from the kitchen window and the front door was open when he and Marie-Thérése arrived. But nothing seems to be missing."

"Do you see the piece of paper anywhere?"

"*Ah, oui*, here it is on the floor." Monique read the number.

Anna hung up and dialed immediately. The call went directly to C-C's voice mail.

"*Excusez-moi, madame.* Your grandfather is out of surgery," the nurse behind the desk informed her. "He's in the intensive care unit just down the corridor. I'll get someone to take you."

When she entered the room, Diamanté was resting quietly.

Anna rose from the wheelchair and stood over the bed. Her grandfather's face was pale as the hospital linens, and the plastic tubing of a cannula delivered oxygen through his nostrils. She took hold of his hand. A few seconds went by before he opened his eyes.

"How are you, *Grand-père?*" she asked.

The old man's breathing was shallow and uneven, but he smiled at her. "A bit groggy. I got it pretty good this time, Anna," he said slowly. His voice was hoarse. She saw him eyeing her arm in the sling.

"It's just a cut," she said. "I'll be okay."

"*Salaud.*" He cursed under his breath. "*L'enculé. Espèce d'idiot!*"

"Listen, *Grand-père*, I spoke with Monique. She has Isabelle safely at the bastide. C-C told me both children were with her, but she doesn't have Luc. What happened? Do you know where he is?"

He stared at her. Then, abruptly, his eyes filled with tears, and he let out a loud cry. His hand grasped hers tightly as he was seized by a violent coughing spasm.

A nurse rushed into the room. "You need to leave, *madame*," she said sternly to Anna, motioning her toward the door. "*Allez-y*. Go now. He must rest."

Diamanté held on tightly to Anna's hand. "I tried…to…stop…him," he said, breathing heavily.

She leaned over him. "Who, *Grand-père*?"

"Manos…said something about Luc being my flesh and blood…how he intended to settle the vendetta."

"What happened then?"

"He was holding the boy, but I don't remember anything after he shot me." He forced back a sob. "Oh, *mon Dieu*, Anna. You must find him…"

Anna's legs felt weak, and her heart was beating fast. "Listen to me, *Grand-père*," she whispered. "Elise will be here any minute. I'm going to try to find out what happened to Luc."

She kissed him on the forehead and left the room with tears streaming down her face.

***

The man in dark glasses seated in the bar of the Ajaccio had listened intently to the phone conversation and then to Elise giving instructions to her sous-chef. He got up, threw some change on the table, and left. Across the square, by the fountain, he made a call.

"He didn't finish him off," he said in Corsican dialect. "He's in the hospital in Grasse. Take the Raven. I'll meet you there."

Chapter Sixty

Georges, Serge, and I sped out of the village and raced onto the main highway.

"We need to find that motorcycle he was riding," I told them. "I have a hunch he's going to try to retrieve it." I recalled Manos's passion for motorcycles on Corsica. "It'll be Italian. That's almost a certainty."

I looked at the passing countryside, my fear growing.

Serge, in the backseat, worried aloud what this rogue would do with the boy.

I suddenly couldn't talk. My heart was beating fast. The temperature in the car seemed stifling. I was perspiring profusely. We passed the place where I had left my father with the farmer and his wife, the owners of the Citroën. There was no one there.

"Slow down," I said. "We should be seeing the motorcycle pretty soon."

Georges reduced speed, and the three of us trained our eyes on both sides of the route.

"That's it," Serge said, suddenly pointing to the shoulder of the oncoming lane.

The bike looked just like the ones Manos preferred: sleek, black, chrome, fast, Italian. I was certain that it was his.

Georges pulled over. "What now?" he asked.

I checked my watch. It was late afternoon. The volume of traffic had diminished. I lowered the passenger-side window. There was a slight breeze and, as always, the constant hum of cicadas.

The cell phone in my pocket vibrated. I opened it and didn't recognize the number.

"*Allô?*"

"C-C?"

"*Amour?*"

"Do you have Luc?"

I hesitated. "*Non*," I said.

Her voice was accusatory. "You don't know where he is, do you?"

I hesitated again. "*Non*," I admitted.

"You lied to me," she snapped. "Why did you tell me Monique had both children when you knew she only had Isabelle?" She was crying and near hysterics. "*Grand-père* said that horrible man took him."

I bit my lip. "The *flics* are searching everywhere. They'll find him. *Je t'assure.* Where are you?"

"My sister-in-law just picked me up at the hospital in Grasse. We're headed to Beausoleil."

"We'll meet you there. I'm with Georges and his brother, at the spot where Manos left his motorcycle. I thought maybe he'd gone back to get it, but apparently *non*."

My eyes stung and my chin was quivering when I terminated the call. I had made a huge miscalculation, which had cost us time. I looked over at Georges, who was watching me.

"Turn around," I said. "We've missed him somehow."

Suddenly, police vehicles, sirens blaring, screeched to a stop in the middle of the road. They shut the traffic down in either direction while a helicopter closed in from overhead.

We got out of the car. I looked up and squinted into the bright sun. A large yellow British government helicopter, similar to the one that returned me to Paris in 1997, was setting down.

Once it was on the ground, the pilot motioned to me. Was it the same man? I blinked my eyes in disbelief, and then I ran toward it. The noise of the rotor was deafening, and I had to brace myself against the downdraft. The door opened, and I climbed in.

"Hi, Doc," I heard. "It's been a while." The pilot shook my hand enthusiastically.

"Geoffrey?"

"The same." He beamed. "*C'est moi.*"

We were in the air immediately.

"But," I stammered, "you are dead, or I heard you were."

"I had to lay low for a while. New bloody name and all that, but everything is back to normal again."

"You mean?"

"Yup. Flo and I've got a couple of little ones, too."

I scratched my head. He was the security guard in the convent in Castagniers. His wife, my nurse, was with us in the helicopter the day we left. My mind raced. If he and Flo were alive, then so must be the double.

He seemed to read my thoughts, opened his mouth to say something, then reconsidered. He was monitoring several screens, and there was audio coming in.

"We had a call from our old friend, Diamanté Loupré-Tigre," he said, changing the subject. "Nicolos Manos is one of us, incidentally, but his record hasn't been very good. Under scrutiny at the moment for suspicion of illegally transporting weapons. Anyway, he apparently ditched the car about a kilometer back. We're tracking the signal from his mobile phone. Should see him on that monitor any moment." He pointed to a screen showing a heavily wooded area.

"How'd you know where to find me?"

"Diamanté used your mobile earlier to call us. He gave specific instructions that you should be involved in the rescue. The phone provided the coordinates. Luckily, you were talking on it just now. Made it easy to locate you."

I was astounded.

"He explained the little boy is your son," Geoffrey continued. He looked over at me sympathetically and said, with more confidence than I felt at the moment, "We'll get him for you, Doc."

I stared out the window. The helicopter was hovering over the trees, making the branches toss violently in the wind. I heard a conversation coming through the speakers.

"You are surrounded. Put your gun down and turn around."

Geoffrey pointed to blurred figures at the top right of the screen.

"That's him," he said. "They've spotted him. Let's see if we can get a clearer picture for the guys below." He maneuvered an electronic gadget and focused in.

I held my breath. It was Manos, and he had my son.

Geoffrey was communicating with the agents on the ground. From what I could gather, they were being told to withhold fire because of Luc. He looked at me to see if I understood. There was static. I watched as Manos tried to make a run for it. Luc, struggling to pull his arm free, lost his footing, and Manos tried to make him stand, then finally picked him up. I wondered about Manos's sanity. How could he ever escape this? They disappeared from the screen.

Geoffrey quickly moved the camera to follow them.

"Look there," he said excitedly as he pointed to the bottom of another screen. An agent with an assault rifle had placed himself directly in Manos's path, behind a wall. "He'll get 'em now, Doc. We're going to get your boy."

The helicopter descended. I watched out the window and saw the agent step from his hiding place. Manos stopped.

We landed. Geoffrey nodded for me to climb out. I saluted him and quickly opened the door. Once I was away from the rotor, a heavily armed police officer grabbed my arm. He handed me a helmet, which I placed on my head.

Chapter Sixty-One

I ran into the wooded area. Just ahead, Nicko was surrounded, his back against a dry stone wall. He held Luc in front of him as a human shield.

My heart beating uncontrollably, I removed the helmet and squatted down a few feet from them.

"*Salut*, Nicko," I said, looking him in the eyes.

He acted surprised to see me.

I took a deep breath to calm myself. "Diamanté is gone. It's what you wanted, isn't it? The vendetta is settled. Let the boy go, Nicko."

He studied my face. His eyes narrowed. "How do I know you're telling me the truth?"

I scratched my head and sighed. "I saw his wound. He won't survive." I saw I was not getting anywhere. "Trust me, Nicko. I am your friend."

"Friends don't blow up friends' yachts," he said bitterly.

So he knew. I shrugged my shoulders. "It was purely a coincidence. We didn't cause that fire. Your explosives did."

His eyes shifted from me to the men surrounding him with rifles. He seemed to be considering something.

"Let my son go," I pleaded in desperation. "Let Luc go."

"Your son?"

"*Oui.*"

On his face, there was almost the playful, inquisitive look of the Nicko I used to know. He cocked his head to the side.

"You didn't tell me you had a son," he said with a wry smile.

I tried to make my voice sound composed and friendly. "Let him go, Nicko. There isn't any reason to hurt him. It's over. Diamanté is dead. Believe me. I know." I was running out of patience. "It's over, Nicko," I repeated, this time in a more forceful voice. "*Laisse-le tomber.* Give it up."

He didn't move. I feared he would try to make a run for it.

"This is pointless," I continued. "What can you possibly gain, *mon ami?*"

I waited for what seemed an interminable amount of time, but I knew it was only seconds. The agents surrounding Nicko and the boy with rifles did not move. The hum of the cicadas was cacophonous.

Finally, Nicko let go of Luc and pushed him in my direction. Dropping his pistol to the ground, he reached for the amulet on the leather cord at his throat and ripped it from his neck. The talisman hurtled through the air, landed against a large boulder, and shattered on impact.

I scooped the little boy into my arms and hugged him to my chest.

Nicko was staring at me.

I watched as the *flics* handcuffed him.

"*Merci,*" I mouthed.

"Your woman," he said. The corner of his upper lip curled into a sneer. "Nice figure." Then he lifted his head back and thrust his chin into the air. "I should have fucked the whore."

The deliberate cruelty in his voice horrified me.

"And you want to know something else?" he yelled over his shoulder as the *flics* pulled him away. "You were never my friend. Hah! MI6 merely assigned me to keep track of you."

As I turned and ran out of the woods with my son in my arms, I realized I was the lucky one. I had so much to live for. Manos had lost everything.

Chapter Sixty-Two

They were gathered around the small television in the kitchen at Beausoleil. Anna watched, breathless, as the news helicopter showed the scene live. C-C was running from the woods carrying Luc. The camera panned in as the two were helped into the helicopter. Monique, Georges, Serge, and Adriana produced loud whoops of joy.

The sudden loud *brrring, brrring, brrring* of the vintage phone on the desk startled them. Monique went over and plucked the receiver from its cradle.

"It's C-C," she said softly as she handed it to Anna.

***

"I have Luc," I said immediately when she answered. "He is unhurt, but a bit shaken, and mostly excited about riding in a helicopter." I was crying, and so was she.

We landed on the grass behind the bastide. I thanked my British friend Geoffrey, the pilot, and shook his hand gratefully.

"Grasse Hospital," I yelled above the rotor's noise. "Get Diamanté out of there *illico presto!*"

He saluted. "Righto, Doc."

"By the way, what happened to the coffin that was in the copter the day we left? The one with André Narbon?"

"At the bottom of the Mediterranean," he said with a smile.

I saw Anna running from the bastide. I helped Luc out of the helicopter and away from the rotor. He jumped up into his mother's waiting arms. She looked at me and held out her hand. I went over and embraced the two of them.

Chapter Sixty-Three

Grasse Hospital

André Narbon *fils* slowly pushed open the hospital room door and sauntered over to the bed.

Diamanté's eyelids fluttered open at the sound of someone in the room. A heavy man stood directly over him. Two close-set, beady black eyes bulged from the fat face. Diamanté groped for the button at the side of the bed that would summon help from the desk in the hall.

"Who are you?" he said to the interloper, his voice nearly gone.

"You don't recognize me, Loupré?" the man said as he yanked the oxygen tube from Diamanté's nostrils. "Don't I look like my father? *Hein,* old man? Your half brother? Remember him? The one you killed?" He put his hands on each side of Diamanté's throat.

Diamanté struggled to rise.

"I just wanted to give my father's killer the evil eye before I have my revenge."

A woman entered the room quietly. She raised a small, jeweled derringer-style pocket pistol, aimed it directly at the intruder's temple, and yelled, "Stop!"

Startled, André Narbon *fils* turned his ugly head.

In that moment, with all the strength left in him, Diamanté wrenched the man's hands away from his throat.

"He didn't kill André. I did," Elise said. She waved the pistol slowly from side to side. "With this."

"Who are you?"

She lifted her chin in her husband's direction. "His wife. My first husband was his brother, Ferdinand. It was during the Second World War. They were members of the Résistance. One night, when they were setting dynamite charges along the railway tracks under a bridge, German soldiers discovered them and opened fire. Ferdinand held the enemy at bay. A lone shot was heard after all was clear. Diamanté went to look for his brother and found him lying facedown in the mud. The back of his head had been blown away. André Narbon was standing over him. It was he who killed Ferdinand, not the Germans. In 1997, he came back to kill Diamanté, too, but *enfin*, it was André who lost his life."

Just then, the door opened. A tall, muscular man in dark glasses entered. With one hand, he snatched the pistol from Elise and pushed her to the floor.

André *fils* smiled. "*Và bé*," he said to his man in Corsican. "Okay. Take her to the Raven."

"Leave her alone." Diamanté gasped for oxygen, his voice nearly gone. "It's me you want. Not her."

Sounds of a commotion came from the hallway, then shouting. The door burst open abruptly. Armed police officers stormed into the room. The Corsican in dark glasses released Elise. André *fils* threw up his arms in surrender.

Gasping for air, Diamanté collapsed back onto the bed.

Part Five

Chapter Sixty-Four

Rome, Italy

Romano and Viola Zennelli were just packing for their departure when Romano's cell phone rang.

"Ah, *bene*," he exclaimed. "It's Adriana." Zenn always looked forward to his daughter's calls. "*Ciao, Bella!*"

"Dad? Have you left for Paris yet?" Adriana's voice sounded frantic.

"We're just packing. The taxi is due here any minute to take us to the airport. What's up?"

"We have to make a change of plans."

Seeing Zenn's eyebrows knit with concern, Viola stopped folding her scarves.

"What's happened?" she whispered.

Zenn stared at his wife as he listened to Adriana explaining that they needed to get Anna and the children out of France as quickly as possible.

"Luc was kidnapped, but he's okay," she said, quickly trying to reassure him. "He wasn't hurt, and he's back with us."

Zenn had to sit down on the bed. His heart beat fast.

"Kidnapped?" he gasped.

"*Madonna mia!*" Vi exclaimed. "Who?"

He put his finger to his lips and mouthed, "Luc."

Vi screamed.

"She says he's okay," he whispered. "Addie," he said into the phone. "What do you want me to do?"

"Are you taking the private jet?"

"Yes. It's waiting for us now at Ciampino."

"Can you possibly pick us up at Nice Airport?"

"Of course. It's just a matter of changing the flight plan on the way to Paris."

"Not Paris, Dad," Adriana said. "We've got to take Anna and the children all the way home to California. Their safety is at stake. We'll explain everything when we see you in Nice. How soon can you be there?"

"I…I don't know. I'll have to consult with the pilot. I'll call you."

"We're near Grasse. It's not a long drive. Let us know when you've taken off, and we'll meet you."

Zenn hung up, shaken. "*Dio mio*," he said to his wife as he began throwing the rest of his clothing into the suitcase. "We're picking them up in Nice. There's been some threat against Anna and the children. Addie didn't say why Luc was kidnapped or how they got him back, but she seemed pretty concerned. Wants us to fly them directly to California."

"I knew Anna shouldn't have taken those children to France," Viola sputtered, putting her hands on her hips. "I told her not to, but she wouldn't listen." She tossed her hands into the air in desperation. "Now look what's happened."

Zenn put his arms around his wife's shoulders. "Let's wait until we know the whole story. At least, *grazie Dio*, they're with Adriana."

Chapter Sixty-Five

Beausoleil

I stood at a distance, watching helplessly, as Anna and Monique packed bags and loaded the children into Georges's sleek black roadster.

Anna and Monique hugged each other; both women were crying. Monique, her nerves shattered, had decided to remain at Beausoleil, rather than accompany them to the airport.

Before she climbed into the front seat, Anna came over to me. She put her hand on my arm and said gently, "I cannot tell you how grateful I am. You saved Luc's life."

I shrugged. "It was your *grand-père*. He called in the special forces."

"Take care of him, will you? He's still in danger, it seems to me."

I nodded.

She leaned in and kissed me softly, *les bis* style, first on the left cheek, then the right. She pulled back a little, looked into my eyes, then kissed me again on my left cheek, this time lingering to nuzzle her cheek against mine for a long moment. We both felt awkward because we knew Adriana was watching us.

I closed my eyes and wondered briefly if Anna would ever tell Mark's family about me.

"May I hug Luc?" I asked, near tears.

She nodded and pressed a folded piece of paper into my hand.

I walked over to the Mercedes, leaned into the backseat, and embraced my son with a heavy heart. I told him I would send him toys.

His eyes sparkled. "Cars?" he asked.

I smiled. We agreed that I would send him cars.

With Georges driving, they took off at high speed, followed closely by Serge and Adriana in the rental car.

Monique's voice came from behind me. "What a ghastly experience," she said.

I turned to look at her. Her eyes were red, and she was dabbing her cheeks with a tissue.

I nodded my head in agreement.

"What will you do now?" she asked.

Good question, I thought. *What kind of future would I have, did I even want to contemplate, without Anna and Luc?*

As I stood there feeling numb, my mobile rang. It was my father. He told me he was at the farmhouse of the elderly couple whose dusty old Citroën Manos had commandeered. I heard him muttering "*nom de Dieu*" over and over as he listened to me describe what had transpired since I left him off.

"I will come pick you up," I said. "Anna and the children have departed."

He gave me directions and told me both the man and the woman were in some need of medical assistance. I remembered that I had my doctor's bag in his car. I told him I would be there shortly. By this time, Monique had returned to the house, so I climbed into my father's old Peugeot sitting in the driveway where Monique left it.

The piece of paper Anna gave me was still in my hand. I unfolded it and saw that she had written her address and a phone number in California. At the bottom, she had drawn a small heart.

With a huge lump in my throat, I started the car and put it in gear. California seemed so far away. How long would it be, I wondered, before I would be able to see them again?

Chapter Sixty-Six

The sun was just setting as I brought the Peugeot to a halt in front of a long rectangular stone building with two sloping roofs. It was a seventeenth-century farmhouse known traditionally in that region as a small *mas* or *mazet*. Because of the fury of the mistral wind, there were no windows on the north side, and the openings on the other three exterior walls were narrow.

My father was waiting for me just outside the massive wooden front door. He threw his arms around my shoulders and hugged me. Then he led me indoors, where the couple, both well into their eighties, were seated at a large carved wooden table in the center of the kitchen. I felt as if I had entered a different period in time. This *petit mas* had the traditional large kitchen on the ground floor. Early in the last century, the space would have been adjacent to where the farm animals were housed. There was a black pot sitting over the glowing embers in the fireplace, and the aroma of stewing meat and vegetables permeated the room.

The man tried to rise, but I indicated for him to remain seated. He relaxed and extended his hand warmly.

"Stéphane," he said. "*Bienvenu*. This is my wife, Irmalin." I set down my medical bag and took their hands.

My father explained that they had walked several kilometers back to the *mas*.

I examined them. Their feet were swollen and blistered. Otherwise, they seemed to be fine.

"You were treated pretty harshly," I said.

They shook their heads in unison. "We were literally thrown from our car!" said the farmer, tossing his arms angrily in the air. His accent was Provençal.

They were very grateful and pressed us to share their evening meal, a true *pot au feu*.

I thanked them for their hospitality but explained that we had to be on our way. My father promised he would return to take them to market day in the nearby village since they did not have their Citroën.

As we departed, my mobile phone rang. It was Anna calling from Nice Airport. She told me they were waiting for the Zennelli plane to arrive.

"It will be a long flight," she said. "At least one refueling stop." She sounded exhausted.

We lingered in bidding each other farewell.

"I love you. I don't want you to leave France," I said.

"I need time," she said.

Chapter Sixty-Seven

Nice Airport

Anna stared at the phone in her hand. Adriana had been watching her. She hadn't understood the conversation as Anna had been speaking entirely in French.

"Who is he?" she asked, a mischievous gleam in her green-gold hazel eyes. "He's very good-looking." She raised an eyebrow. "How long have you known him?"

Anna studied her sister-in-law's face. "Can you keep a secret, Addie?" she asked.

***

Anna finished telling Adriana about her relationship with C-C just as an agent from airport security arrived to announce that the Zennelli plane had touched down.

"No need to awaken the children yet," he told them, explaining that the plane was to be refueled and he would return when it was time to board.

Adriana searched in her briefcase and pulled out an envelope. "Wait to open it on the plane," she said, handing it over to Anna.

Anna looked surprised when she saw her name written across the front. The handwriting was Mark's. "But what is it?"

"Mark left it for you," Adriana explained. "It was in the office safe along with a letter of instruction, for my eyes only. In the event of his accidental death, it said, I was to give this to you. He specifically stated that I was to wait until I felt you were ready. A few months, but no more than a year. He briefly explained about Luc so I'd understand. It's one of the main reasons I decided to make this trip."

Anna smoothed her trembling fingers over the front of the envelope, then placed it in the outside pocket of her carry-on.

"He left something else for me." Adriana sighed. "A potential bombshell with regards to the firm."

Anna looked up.

"He was concerned about a client. Dad's client in Strasbourg, to be specific. As you probably knew, Mark had more and more been drawn into helping secure international financing for the films Dad's company was producing. It made sense, of course. Mark could spot legal issues. With the Strasbourg client, he was suspicious of something, though."

"He never mentioned anything like that to me," Anna said, her brow furrowed.

"It came as a total surprise to me. I went through his files, and I did find serious discrepancies, so I arranged the meeting in Strasbourg. Now I've met the key players. When I get home, I'm going to launch a full-scale investigation. The damned thing could spiral out of control on us. It could even mean a financial meltdown for Dad. The mystery in all this is that I still don't know exactly how much Mark knew, or what he was planning to ultimately do about it." She smiled. "He always just described it as a bunch of bullshit."

Anna laughed. "One of his favorite words."

With her fingers, Adriana combed through her long golden-blonde hair, gathered it into a ponytail, and twisted a hair band around it. "Do you think he had a premonition when he wrote those letters? Seems strange, doesn't it?"

Anna nodded. Seeing the agent approaching, she stood to gather her things. "Time to wake up the children," she said.

Chapter Sixty-Eight

After she had settled the children in, and the plane had taken off, Anna quietly opened the envelope.

The letter was written on the firm's fine linen stationery, in Mark's familiar small, uneven handwriting, a sloppy mix of cursive and print. She ran her fingers over the embossed letters centered at the top of the page:

Zennelli and Zennelli, Attorneys at Law
M.A. Zennelli, Senior Partner

Dear gorgeous, it began. She could hear his voice. In the months since 9/11, it was what she'd missed most. Hearing him tell her how much he loved her, calling her "gorgeous."

Dear gorgeous,
 If Adriana has given you this letter, something has happened to me. I have written in my instructions that she should determine the appropriate time and place to deliver it. Adriana and you are close, and I trust her judgment on that.
 First of all, I want you to know that I love you more than anything. You are my life, my partner, my best friend. I will always love you, you and Luc.

> *Which brings me to the reason I am writing this. You should know that I spent some time searching for Luc's father. This was when we were first married and you were pregnant. At the time, my thinking was we would notify him when the baby was born. The search took more effort than I thought. When I finally had a name (his new name), Luc was here, and I had adopted the boy as my own. I couldn't bring myself to do anything more with the information.*
>
> *Anna, I didn't withhold the name intentionally, but selfishly. I wanted you and Luc for my own family, and we were so happy, the three of us. I imagined the guy you called C-C not wanting to be found, and, conveniently, decided he might even have established a new life, with a wife and a family. After all, he* was *involved in some sort of shady undercover operation by the British government. I never was able to find out what exactly, but that in itself made it easy for me to justify my decision.*

Anna paused and listened to the drone of the airplane's engines.

The flight attendant brought her a cup of tea and set milk and cookies on a tray for Luc. He and the baby had fallen fast asleep. Anna took a sip of the tea and turned to the second page.

> *Which brings me back to why I decided to write this letter to you, gorgeous. I got to thinking one day. What if something happened to me? Luc would be left without a father! Christ! When his real father might even still be alive!*
>
> *So, here is the conclusion I came to, LOVE OF MY LIFE: If I have passed, either by natural causes or accidentally,*

and you are able and willing, find the man who goes by the name of Charles Guilbert (aka the former Charles-Christian Gérard). It won't be easy tracking him down, I suspect. But, if you succeed, let him know he has a son.

Of course, this all depends on Luc's age, and I know you will consider the circumstances carefully.

This last part is the most difficult for me to write.

If you still love the man, and he still loves you, and you two are able to work it out, for Luc's sake, then I encourage you both to do so, with my (albeit reluctant) blessing.

With all my love and devotion forever,
Your Mark

Anna stared out the window of the plane. The layer of white, puffy clouds below created an unworldly sensation, as if she were caught between Earth and the afterworld. This letter from Mark, written before he knew he was going to be a father to Isabelle, had taken her by surprise, but it somehow felt right. A sudden calm came over her. His words had both reassured her and told her to get on with what she had known all along she had to do.

Chapter Sixty-Nine

Anna walked to the front of the plane, passing Adriana and her mother-in-law lounging in flat, bed-like seats. She pointed toward the compartment ahead, raised her eyebrows, and mouthed "Zenn?"

Adriana smiled and nodded encouragingly.

The forward compartment of the private jet was reserved for Romano's use. It was mainly his office. A large desk provided ample room for him to work, and a bar stocked with wine and liquor stood opposite for when he entertained clients and guests. She found him seated in a luxuriously padded swivel seat staring out a window. She slipped into the matching seat next to him and swiveled it in his direction.

"You're not sleeping?" she asked, leaning forward and taking his hand in hers.

He looked startled.

"No. I never do anymore," he said.

She had to gulp back a sob. His warm hazel eyes were so much like Mark's. For a moment, the man's stark white hair turned a sandy color, and an older, more mature version of Mark appeared. She blinked and willed away the thought.

"When I do," he continued, "I always have the same dream. I…I have this image…It's Mark…in free fall…" He pinched the bridge of his nose with his thumb and forefinger in an effort to repress his emotions.

"This past year has been difficult," she said. "I've had similar dreams. A plane. Fire. Explosions. The towers. I always wake up in a panic."

The airplane hit mild turbulence, and the Fasten Seat Belt sign lit with a two-toned chime.

Zenn looked out the window, then over at her. "You know what Mark was doing at the World Trade Center that morning?"

She shook her head. "I guess I assumed it was some important Hollywood business of yours."

He nodded, then sighed. "It was. He was sealing a financial deal for a client of mine whose movie I planned to back." He put his hand on his forehead.

Anna looked at him compassionately. The ebullient, self-confident man who had always been the life of the party seemed shell-shocked.

"I've got to tell you, Anna. I blame myself every day. I'll go to my grave blaming myself."

"I don't hold you responsible," she said, patting his hand. "You couldn't have known what was going to happen. No one did."

"The irony of it, Anna, was that the movie was going to be one of those sci-fi thrillers about the destruction of New York City…by alien invaders." He chuckled bitterly. "After September Eleventh, we had to rewrite the screenplay, find another city to destroy."

"Speaking of New York," she said, "I've been resisting going with you for the anniversary. I...I just didn't know if I would be able to deal with it."

He looked up.

"Now, I've decided I'll go, if you still want me to, that is."

His immediate reaction was to wrap his arms around her in exaltation. Then a confused look came over his face.

"Why would I not want you to go? *Dio mio!* It's the news I've been hoping to hear."

Anna handed him Mark's letter. "After you've read this, I have a long story to tell you."

Chapter Seventy

The month of August ended, and I returned to Corsica just long enough to close out my apartment and resign from my position at the hospital. I brought Diamanté's Fiat back to Castagniers and then headed to Paris to retrieve my own Mercedes. While there, I submitted all the paperwork to reestablish my identity as Charles-Christian Gérard.

Then I sent a long letter to Anna, a love letter. *Amour, mon amour, ma chère,* it began. I reminded her of the love we had shared and asked her, pleaded with her, to consider becoming my wife. I signed it, *de l'homme qui t'aimera toujours avec tout son coeur,* "from the man who will always love you with all his heart."

Next, I sent gifts for Luc and the baby.

For two weeks, I was in constant anguish, despairing at the thought that I might have lost her for good. Then came a short e-mail message from her saying she needed more time and, by the way, Luc adored the toy cars I had sent. She added that she and her in-laws had been to New York City for the difficult first anniversary of the 9/11 attacks. This last piece of information only served to distress me more.

But for Diamanté's deteriorating health, I would have been on the next plane to Los Angeles. He had never fully recovered from the injuries Nicko inflicted upon him. In addition, the cough, about which I had been concerned, worsened. While he was in the hospital, it was discovered that he had lung cancer, apparently the result of chemicals and secondary smoke he had inhaled decades before as a young man working in the metallurgical factory in Marseilles.

We brought him home to the Ajaccio and installed him in the upstairs suite, where he was officially in hospice. At the same time, I began telephoning Anna daily to give her an update on his condition. *Mais oui!* I have to admit it was an excuse to hear her voice. Occasionally, I also heard my son in the background, which warmed my heart.

By early October, Diamanté's condition was becoming extremely grave. I told Anna it was urgent that she come to France as soon as she could to bid her grandfather *adieu*. Alarmed, she agreed and made plans immediately. To Diamanté's delight, and mine, she arrived with the children soon after. Filled with joy, I gathered the three in my arms and showered them all with hugs and kisses.

Diamanté, who had watched the happy reunion in front of the Ajaccio from the upstairs balcony off his bedroom, wasted little time in calling Anna and me to his bedside for a private *tête-à-tête*. His demeanor serious, breathing heavily and gasping for breath, he told us bluntly that he knew we loved each other and he wanted to see us together before he died.

That evening, in the rose garden, after the children had been put to bed, I told her once again how much I loved her and asked her if she would consent to marry me. To my utter joy, she agreed.

A few days later, we were married in a civil ceremony in the mayor's tiny office in the town hall in Castagniers. Monique and Georges stood up for us. Serge, Georges's brother the screenwriter, and his new girlfriend, none other than Anna's sister-in-law, Adriana, flew in from Los Angeles.

In his wheelchair, and breathing with the aid of a portable oxygen concentrator, a smiling Diamanté watched the ceremony with Luc perched on his lap, while Elise, sitting by his side, took charge of beautiful, curly-headed Isabelle.

During the reception, at the Ajaccio, of course, Diamanté toasted us and assured us he could die a happy man now that we were together. And, sadly, that happened just two weeks later. We had postponed any plans for a wedding trip so we could be with him until the end. Elise, Anna, and I accompanied his body on his final journey to Corsica, where we saw him laid to rest in the Loupré family tomb in Speloncato, next to his beloved son, Anna's father.

***

Some time later, in going through Diamanté's things, Elise found a tattered old leather journal, written during the war, in his native Corsican. The pages had yellowed, and the ink had faded, but it was legible. Luckily, my father was still around to translate it for us. It began with the reason for his leaving Corsica at the age of fifteen, and finally provided the missing piece of the puzzle: the explanation for why he had not dared risk returning to the island for so many years. We were all astonished to learn that it was he who had planned, and deliberately carried out, his stepfather's murder.

According to Diamanté's journal, every morning at dawn, Larenzu Narbon was in the habit of going for a horseback ride in the *maquis*. The morning Diamanté planned to depart, he rose early and waited, hidden in the dense underbrush, with his rifle ready. When the horse and rider came upon a massive dead tree trunk in the middle of the path, they paused. It was then that the young Diamanté got off a clear shot. Old Narbon fell off his horse and hit his head on a large rock. After determining that the man was dead, Diamanté sneaked back to the house, finished packing his things, bid farewell to his mother, and took off for Marseilles. He had single-handedly avenged his own father's death on behalf of the Loupré family, and freed his mother from the terrible abuse she had suffered. The year was 1939, and the stage had been set for the next act in the blood war. It was now the responsibility of Larenzu's only son, André Narbon, to murder his father's killer. André wrongfully assumed that Ferdinand, Diamanté's older brother, had carried out the deed. Somehow, he learned along the way that it was really Diamanté he wanted. It was not clear when he had learned the truth, but in 1998, he arrived in Castagniers intending to kill Diamanté at last. It was he who lost his life instead.

Which advanced the vendetta to the year 2002. André's son, André Narbon *fils*, was arrested in Diamanté's hospital room in Grasse, but apparently managed to buy his way out of the situation. As he headed home to Calvi that night, his private helicopter was caught in a violent storm over the Mediterranean, and he was never seen again.

And Nicolos Manos? The last living person of the Narbon family was charged with attempted murder and kidnapping. While he awaited trial, the results of the investigation into *The Blue Amulet*'s sinking were revealed. The sole surviving member of the crew had testified that Nicko abandoned ship just before it blew up. In addition, there were reports that he was smuggling weapons and other contraband for Basque terrorist groups as well as the Corsican mafia. Presumed guilty under the *Code Napoléon*, and unable to prove his innocence, he was convicted of all charges and sent to Fresnes Prison, just south of Paris, where he remains today.

The vendetta came to an end with the result being the near mutual extinction of both families. There were no more Narbons or Louprés left on Corsica.

***

It is now 2004. Anna and I divide our time between California and the house in Castagniers, which Diamanté willed back to us on his death. We spend holidays and summers there, and the school year in Laguna Beach, where Luc has started kindergarten. When we are in California, Anna writes, and I volunteer my time with Médecins Sans Frontières, which satisfies my urge to travel, although I am rarely gone for long from my family.

My father, "Papa Jacques" to Luc, has sold his *resto* in Saint-Florent and stayed on permanently in Castagniers to run the Ajaccio's operations. His new friends, whom he visits often in their farmhouse near Grasse, still have their old, dusty yellow Citroën.

Elise spends her time welcoming guests as *la grande dame* of the Ajaccio, where she has taken up permanent residence.

The Zennelli clan has accepted my existence as Anna's husband. Romano, especially, seemed apprehensive to begin with. The first time I met him, he took me out by the pool of his Bel Air estate and divulged that Anna had confided my story to him. Then he asked me point-blank what my involvement had been in the British cover-up operation. I answered, as I had been instructed to do, that the inquest would officially conclude Princess Diana died in the accident in Paris. Despite the conspiracy theories, and the tabloid photo taken of a Diana look-alike staring from an open second-story window inside an old stone convent in Southern France, the double never existed. I told him I had lost four years of my life to a piece of fiction. He laughed, slapped me on the shoulder, and said he'd like to make a movie of that someday.

In reality, I chanced across Diana's double earlier this spring by sheer coincidence. During an evening stroll along the beach in California, a woman in a wheel chair approached me from the opposite direction, pushed along slowly by a tall, lanky man with a chiseled chin. As the pair drew closer, a familiar face glanced up at me from under her big floppy beach hat. Our eyes met for a moment in mutual recognition, then I continued on my way, reassured that the *saudade*, the deep longing and emptiness in both our lives, was gone.

I have my identity back, and I am no longer paranoid about someone following me. I do have a new assumed name, however. Luc has begun to call me "Daddy."

Anna's latest novel, a thriller titled *The Tale of the Evil Eye*, has just made the best-seller lists.

She and I dance whenever we hear a waltz.

ACKNOWLEDGMENTS

My heartfelt thanks to Peter Berkos, Lillian Balinfante Herzberg, Morry Shechet, Brae Wyckoff, Mark Carlson, Rosalie Kramer, Terry Ambrose, Debra Friend, and the late Karl Bell, all members of the Rancho Bernardo Writers Group in San Diego, California, whose tough critique, diplomatic suggestions, sound advice, and steadfast support made this story better. A special thank-you also to Glynda Bockler and Jean Sommers, who so graciously read the manuscript and provided extensive comments. Finally, *merci beaucoup* to my husband, Denny, whose love and encouragement I truly value, and to our daughter, Kirsten, for her enthusiasm and belief.

Made in the USA
Charleston, SC
21 June 2012